Hope

for

Christmas

by

Elizabeth Maddrey

Scripture quoted by permission. Quotations designated (NIV) are from THE HOLY BIBLE: NEW INTERNATIONAL VERSION®. NIV®. Copyright © 1973, 1978, 1984 by Biblica. All rights reserved worldwide.

Cover design by Jennifer Zemanek of Seedlings Design Studio

Published in the United States of America by Elizabeth Maddrey
www.ElizabethMaddrey.com

Publisher's Note: This novel is a work of fiction. Names, characters, places, and incidents are either products of the author's imagination or used fictitiously. All characters are fictional, and any similarity to people living or dead is purely coincidental.

Other Books by Elizabeth Maddrey

Peacock Hill Romance Series
A Heart Restored
A Heart Reclaimed
A Heart Realigned

Arcadia Valley Romance – Baxter Family Bakery Series
Loaves & Wishes (in *Romance Grows in Arcadia Valley*)
Muffins & Moonbeams
Cookies & Candlelight
Donuts & Daydreams

The 'Operation Romance' Series
Operation Mistletoe
Operation Valentine
Operation Fireworks
Operation Back-to-School

The 'Taste of Romance' Series
A Splash of Substance
A Pinch of Promise
A Dash of Daring
A Handful of Hope
A Tidbit of Trust

The 'Grant Us Grace' Series
Joint Venture
Wisdom to Know
Courage to Change
Serenity to Accept

The 'Remnants' Series:
Faith Departed
Hope Deferred
Love Defined

Stand alone novellas
Kinsale Kisses: An Irish Romance
Luna Rosa (part of A Tuscan Legacy)

For the most recent listing of all my books, please visit my website.

For my mother, thank you for always believing in me.

1

Cyan Hewitt stared out at the waves of the Pacific Ocean. The pebbly beach on Whidbey Island wasn't comfortable for sitting, so he'd found himself doing a lot of standing on mornings when the sea called to him. He burrowed his hands into the kangaroo pocket of the hoodie he'd gotten in college. It was the one piece of spirit wear he owned, and he hadn't purchased it because he loved the school, but because he'd been cold and they'd been discounted.

A lot of the things in his life were like that. Convenient, useful, but not particularly meaningful.

He sighed and turned away from the water.

He was a lot like that, and the lack of meaning was like a constant itch under his skin that nothing could scratch.

His sister, Azure, said it was because he needed Jesus. His grandparents, with whom he'd recently initiated contact, hinted at the same thing. They weren't as "pound your face in it" as Azure, but then, there weren't many people in the world like his sister.

Cyan smiled. Of his siblings, she was his favorite. Which was why her words had taken root in his heart. Did he need Jesus? Would faith really quiet his restless heart?

Thanksgiving was next week. He'd planned to swing south and see his parents' new house. The fact that they'd settled down in one spot didn't surprise him as much as it seemed to amaze his other siblings. Why wouldn't they? They'd seen everything they wanted to see, been everywhere they wanted to be. Why keep roaming when the road stopped calling?

It had stopped calling him years ago, but he'd continued the family tradition of wandering simply because he hadn't wanted to be the first to bow to convention, or however his parents would've phrased it had they not been the ones to start the trend. Now they were homeowners, and Azure was heading back to southern Virginia and the man she'd fallen in love with—a man as tied down as they came, from what his sister told him—which meant maybe now he could park somewhere himself.

The question became where?

He didn't particularly want to see his parents.

That was horrible, of course, but being around them amplified the itch under his skin.

Cyan sighed and climbed the hill, away from the water, to the beach house he was house sitting. The owners would be back tomorrow, so he'd clear out today. It wouldn't be the first time he'd gotten in his car without a destination in mind.

If he was lucky, though, it might be the last.

Homey chores took him through the morning. With his car packed and the key turned in to the house sitting agency, Cyan frowned at the map. South. But to where?

Azure's number popped up on his cell, and he smiled. Maybe his sister would have an idea.

"Hey, Az."

"Hey. You on the road yet?" The noise of her old truck's engine was audible over the connection. How did she stand driving around in a vintage car without the creature comforts modern engineering provided?

"Almost. Trying to figure out where to go. How close to Virginia are you?"

"I've still got another two, three days before I'm home. Go see the grandparents. You'll like them."

Home? Had he ever heard his sister use that word and mean something other than the vintage camper that served as her mobile tiny home as she moved around from job to job? It was weird—and nice—to think of her with someone important in her life. He'd have to meet the man at some point. "Or I could come to Virginia, too, and see if this guy's good enough for you."

She laughed. "He is. And I'm serious. You'd love their ranch. They have horses."

"Why would I love that?" It wasn't that he disliked animals. He'd considered, at one time, becoming a veterinarian. Until he'd realized just how much extra school that entailed. No thank you. But he knew next to nothing about horses.

"Trust me on this. Betsy—Grandma—was talking about her Hatch chile stuffed turkey that they always serve for Thanksgiving dinner. If I didn't need to get back to Matt, I would've stayed just to try it myself. They're great. You told me that yourself. Why don't you want to meet them in person?"

"I do. They are. It's just—" What? What was it? "Wasn't it weird?"

"Maybe a little. But like you said, they're good people. And they love us, Cy. Even having never met us. Go to New Mexico."

"You don't think I should head to Arizona? See Mom and Dad?"

Azure sighed. "If you want. They'd love to see you, too."

"But you think I'd be better off at the grandparents'?"

"I think you should do what you want. I just know Wayne and Betsy would love to meet you in person."

He laughed. There was the sister he knew and loved. "What do they do at the ranch? Would I be in the way?"

"I'm not sure they do a ton anymore. Wayne wants to retire. They seem to have a solid group of people working for them. They have horses and do riding lessons. I think they board horses for people in the area as well. And there are cabins—Betsy said something about camps of some sort during the summer."

It sounded interesting. "Still warm there?"

"Um. No. They're on a mesa and near good skiing. They'd already had some snow this year and were expecting more. It's not at all like what I picture when I think of New Mexico. But then, I'm not sure I knew what to picture."

Skiing was fun. He hadn't been in a while, but the times he'd been he'd enjoyed it. "Maybe I'll do that. Not like I can't leave if it's weird."

"There you go." Azure chuckled. "Let me know what you think, okay?"

"Yeah, I can do that. Thanks, Az." Cyan ended the call and pulled up the map on his phone. He studied the route, nodded, and pointed his car toward the Interstate. It'd take close to twenty-two hours of driving to get there, so he might as well get started.

Cyan bumped down the dirt road toward the ranch entrance. *Rancho de Esperanza.* He'd looked it up. It meant

Ranch of Hope. That seemed right in line with how he'd categorized his grandparents in their increasingly frequent conversations. They were full of hope and love and, what was it? Optimism, maybe? It wouldn't bother him if some of that rubbed off on him. He could use it.

He'd stopped for the night in Durango, Colorado, not wanting to show up at the ranch in the middle of the night. He hadn't let them know he was coming. He hadn't been completely sure he *was* coming. Part of him still thought he'd be better off heading to see his parents in Arizona. Maybe swinging down to see Indigo and her husband, too. But curiosity about his grandparents, especially now that Azure had met them, swung the pendulum toward New Mexico.

Hopefully they'd be glad to see him.

A big, single-story, adobe house sprawled in the center of the view. The road curved around to form a driveway and split off leading toward wooden structures behind. Those had to be the stables, didn't they? A split-rail fence made a circle to one side. Someone worked with a horse on a long lead inside it.

Out of his depth. He was completely and utterly out of his depth.

With a deep breath, he pulled his battered station wagon to a stop in front of the house and climbed out. If they didn't want him to stay, he'd head back into Taos. It wasn't a big deal.

It *felt* like one.

Terracotta pavers made a path to the door. It was all so Southwestern, Cyan couldn't stop the smile as he pushed the doorbell.

Footsteps—most likely female from the clicking sound they made—approached, and the wooden door swung open. Cyan had expected an older woman, maybe carrying an extra ten pounds, with silver hair. The woman in front of him was young—thirty on the outside—and had a sassy cap of short black hair on her head. Her skin was tan, and she was tall enough to look him in the eye. Her expression blended curiosity and annoyance.

He was gaping. Cyan dragged his thoughts together— he'd seen beautiful women before, so there was no rational reason for this one to be affecting him—and cleared his throat. "I'm looking for Betsy. Or Wayne. Hewitt."

She lifted a single eyebrow. "And you are?"

"Cyan. Also Hewitt. Their grandson?"

The woman blinked and the tiniest hint of a frown formed on her lips. "I'll see if Betsy's available for you."

The door shut in his face. Cyan blew out a breath. He hadn't missed the implication that Betsy might not be willing to see him. There was no reason for that. At least, not that he knew of. Did they have people claiming to be their grandchild show up every day?

The door was flung open, and a woman who bore a much closer resemblance to what he'd pictured flew through it, her arms extended. "Cyan? You're here! Why didn't you tell us you were coming?"

He chuckled and returned her hug, patting her shoulders and trying to ease back. "I wasn't sure I was until this morning."

"Still, you could've called. Or texted." Her eyes danced. "I'm getting better at texting. Where'd you come from today?"

"Durango. It's not a bad drive."

"You must be famished. It's nearly lunch anyway. Let's go see if Maria has something you can eat. Come in.

Wayne's going to be so excited you're here. He's in town this morning." She looped her arm through his and dragged him into the house while she spoke.

"It's okay that I came?" Cyan took in the warm, wood floors and southwestern art on the walls as they crossed the entry hall and a huge open living room before taking two steps up to a tiled kitchen.

"It's more than okay. It's a delight. You sit here." Betsy patted a stool at the counter and frowned. "Now, where did Maria get to?"

"I'm right here." The woman who'd answered the door at first stepped out of an alcove. Pantry? She flicked a glance at Cyan and her mouth turned down. "He's really your grandson?"

"Don't let her manner fool you, Maria's as sweet as they come once she gets to know you. She just doesn't like being interrupted when she's fixing lunch." Betsy patted Cyan's hand and beamed at Maria. "Of course he is. He's the spitting image of his father, too."

Now it was Cyan's turn to frown. People who knew his dad said that. A lot. But it wasn't something he focused on. He loved his dad, but he didn't want anyone thinking he was a cookie cutter replica. "There's some of my mom in me as well."

"Oh honey, of course there is." Betsy studied his face. "I meant it as a compliment. Anyway, Maria, meet my grandson Cyan. Cyan, this is Maria Sanchez. She keeps us running, fed, and organized."

"I'm the housekeeper. That's what she's trying to say." Maria offered a tight smile. "One more for lunch?"

"If you made enough, otherwise I can fix him a sandwich."

"I have a big pot of posole on, there's plenty. Hope you like green chiles." Maria took a wooden spoon and stirred the enormous stewpot that steamed on the stove.

"I don't know whether I do or not, but I guess I'll find out. I appreciate you feeding me." Cyan clasped his hands together on the counter.

"How long can you stay?" Betsy slid onto the stool beside him. "I know Wayne will want a chance to meet you."

Cyan shrugged. "I don't have any plans. I can work from wherever I am as long as there's internet."

"That must be nice. What do you do?" Maria tapped the spoon and set it aside.

"I do computer security consulting. Basically, the organization I work for is hired by other companies to make sure their networks aren't easily breached from outside. Sometimes I need to go on site for a day or two, but generally I can work with the IT people they have and do everything else remotely. I like the flexibility."

Maria's smile was a little looser this time. "Who wouldn't? Lunch is about ready, Betsy, if you want to go ring the bell."

Cyan watched his grandmother hop off the stool and stride from the room. Grandmother. It was still odd to wrap his mind around that. He focused his attention on Maria and enjoyed the sensation of his heart speeding up. She was pretty, and a little prickly, but that could be fun in the right circumstances. "What got you into housekeeping?"

She laughed and tugged the ladle from a tall canister holding all manner of serving implements. "I don't think anyone goes into housekeeping on purpose. I was halfway through my undergraduate degree when I got pregnant. I dropped out of college and ended up here. I used to come up here for riding lessons when I was younger, camp, too, with the church. I accepted Jesus at a bonfire one night right here on the ranch. In many ways, Wayne and Betsy have been better to me than anyone in my family, so I knew I could come here, lick my wounds, and figure out what was next with no judgment. Calvin's seven now, and this is the only home he's known. Even if I wanted to leave, I couldn't do that to him."

She had a son. A seven-year-old. That made her about his age—within a year or two certainly. Surprisingly, the fact that she had a child didn't immediately dampen his interest like it normally would. "Can I ask you a question?"

"Sure." Maria didn't look up from ladling thick stew into bowls.

"How does it work to do the Jesus thing, have a kid, and not be married?" His sister, Azure, was always slipping little comments about Jesus into their conversations. So were his grandparents, for that matter. While he'd never been adamantly opposed to the idea of God like his dad, he hadn't seen the question as something that mattered to him until recently.

Maria sighed and set the ladle aside. "You're not a Christian."

It wasn't a question, but he still felt compelled to answer. "No. My sister Azure would say she's working on me."

That got a tiny smile to flitter across her lips. "Good for her. I knew I liked her when she visited last week. As for your question, I guess the short answer is: it shouldn't. But, thankfully, God has grace and forgives our sin when we repent. I messed up, but God redeemed me."

Cyan nodded. Maybe step one was accepting someone else's definition of sin. Why did sex fall into that category? If it was something God made, then why was it sin? He could get behind calling lying and stealing sin, most of the time. Of course, there were exceptions, weren't there? What if the truth was more damaging? He watched Maria slide a huge pan of golden cornbread out of the oven. Before he could decide on what to say next, three men clomped into the room and started pulling out stools. Skipping behind them, chattering a million miles an hour to Betsy, was a little boy who was the spitting image of Maria.

"Everyone, before we say grace and dig into that amazing smelling lunch, I'd like to introduce you to my grandson, Cyan. Cyan, these are the guys. They handle the horses and the upkeep on the fences, that sort of thing. I'll let them introduce themselves while you eat. And this," she rested her hand on the boy's head, "is Calvin."

Calvin grinned and scampered to the only empty stool at the kitchen bar. "Hi."

"Hi." Cyan glanced at the group and searched for words.

"Let's pray." Betsy shot him a wink before bowing her head.

Right. Bow his head. Eyes closed, too, right? He darted a look around before squeezing his eyelids shut and wondering again why he'd come here.

2

Maria kicked off her shoes and collapsed onto the couch in the little two-bedroom cabin she shared with Calvin. Betsy had shooed her out of the main house after she'd finished cleaning up from lunch. There were still chores to do, but they'd keep. They always did. If Betsy wanted time with her grandson without someone else around, well, that was her prerogative. Cyan—and wasn't that an odd name?—was someone who seemed like it'd be fun to spend time with. Not that she was looking for any sort of relationship. It didn't—wouldn't—matter that something about him set off pleasant little tingles in her stomach. And if she was thinking about tingles, it's good she had a little break. She didn't have time for tingles.

With Calvin on half-days for the start of the week and then off Wednesday through Friday for Thanksgiving, extra time with him was something she'd savor.

If she could get him away from the horses.

Chuckling at her horse-crazy boy, she dragged his backpack closer and dug through the mess to find the red folder that was supposed to hold any important papers, like permission slips and notes from the teacher. Of course, she'd found both of those things floating amongst the other ephemera in his bag before, so she usually tried to go through and sort everything at least once a week. With the extra time this afternoon, she might as well.

The red folder held a history test she needed to sign— a C minus. Maria dug in the bottom of the backpack for a pen and signed across the top. She couldn't blame him for missing some of the dates. After a while, they all started to blend together, and she hadn't yet found any of those dates critical to her adult life. Still, she'd try to make sure he studied more.

The teacher had also included a note asking if Calvin had been getting enough sleep lately as he'd been acting lethargic off and on for the past couple of days.

Maria frowned and looked up as the front door opened. "Hey, baby. You're done with the horses already?"

Calvin nodded as he kicked his shoes toward the basket where they were supposed to go. He shuffled over to the couch and slumped onto it. "You found the test?"

"I did. It's signed and everything. We'll study harder next time, okay? But a C's still okay." Maria ruffled his hair and surreptitiously slid her hand onto his forehead. He didn't feel warm. "You feeling all right? Mrs. Perez says you've been tired a lot at school."

He shrugged.

Maria sighed. Sometimes getting her son to talk was like pulling teeth. "Are you sleeping okay?"

"I guess."

"If that changes, you let me know?"

He nodded. "Okay if I go read in my room for a while?"

Maria paused. Calvin was a good reader, but it wasn't usually something he asked to do. Generally, she had to cajole—or threaten—him into it. "Of course. You're still going to help me decorate the main house on Friday, right? You know how Mr. and Mrs. Hewitt like their Christmas decorations."

He gave a weak smile. "Yeah. Maybe it'll snow and we can go cut down the trees."

"We'll cut the trees either way, but snow would make getting out there more fun." Her boy loved the snowmobile. Wayne loved riding on it with Calvin. It was win-win. She watched him drag himself toward his bedroom. Maybe she'd talk him into letting her take his temperature anyway, just to be safe.

Drumming her fingers on her legs, she grabbed her cell phone and punched in Mrs. Perez's number.

"Hello?"

"Mrs. Perez? It's Maria Sanchez. I saw your note about Calvin seeming off—could you tell me how long you feel like he's been that way?"

"Sure. I wasn't trying to alarm you, it's just so unlike Calvin that I thought I'd mention it. Maybe since last Wednesday?"

Had she noticed? She'd been so busy, knowing Thanksgiving kicked off the start of the Christmas season on the ranch, and Wayne and Betsy liked to do it up. They had sleigh rides, with or without snow, and caroling sing-a-longs by a huge bonfire every weekend leading up to Christmas. It was worth it, but it was a lot of extra work for everyone. Consequently, she tried to get as many of the once-monthly chores done *before* the madness kicked off. "Okay. I can't say I saw anything, but I do today. I'll take his temperature before dinner. Is there anything going around school?"

"Just the usual sniffles, nothing major. You know, if you need to keep him home tomorrow, it's not like he's going to miss anything. I'm not assigning any homework over Thanksgiving other than thirty minutes of reading each night."

Maria smiled. "That's awesome. Thanks."

Mrs. Perez chuckled. "You're welcome. Tell Calvin I hope he's feeling better soon."

"I will. Thanks. Have a good Thanksgiving."

"You, too. Oh. Are the usual Christmas celebrations starting up at the ranch next week?"

"That's the plan."

"Fantastic. Mr. Perez owes me a sleigh ride, and there's nowhere nicer than Esperanza."

"I don't disagree. We'll look forward to seeing you one night. Bye." Maria ended the call and blew out a breath. Almost a week. She headed to the bathroom but found the door closed. He'd gone to the bathroom in the big house after lunch, before heading to the horses. She tapped. "You okay?"

The door swung open and Calvin nodded. "I'm fine."

"Since you're here, hang on. I want to take your temperature."

He sighed but went back in, flipping the toilet closed and sitting on it.

Maria smiled and stuck the thermometer under his tongue. One of these days she'd upgrade to the ear kind that was practically instantaneous, but for now, the digital thermometer was good enough. After a minute, it beeped. "Normal. Maybe it's just a cold. Tell me if something starts hurting?"

"Yeah, Mom, I said I would."

She winced at his tone. She probably ought to correct him. It wasn't super respectful. On the other hand, he *had* said that and she needed to let it go rather than spinning into worry over something that was probably nothing. "Okay. Go read."

"I'm gonna get some water. Can I take it in my room?"

"Yeah, okay." Normally, food and drink were supposed to stay in the kitchen or at the little table they used for meals when they weren't in the main house. But it was just water.

Maria headed back to the couch to dig through the rest of Calvin's backpack. Then maybe she'd spend an hour or so reading herself before heading next door to start supper.

Maria switched on her music streaming app and hesitated. Was it too soon for Christmas music? She tapped the station. It was close enough. The guys didn't usually come for dinner, so it'd just be the Hewitts—all three of them—Calvin, and her. Each of the three ranch hands had their own cabin like hers, complete with a roomy enough kitchen, so it wasn't like it was a hardship to have to fend for themselves. Maria liked the cozier, family-like feeling of dinners with the Hewitts.

Tonight was a simple casserole of chicken, green chiles, rice, and cheese. She'd throw it together, get it in the oven, and then have another hour before she needed to do anything else. Maybe Calvin would be up for a board game.

"Need any help?"

Maria turned at the voice and nearly dropped the casserole dish. Cyan was light on his feet, she hadn't heard his approach. "No. I'm good. Thanks."

"Mind if I watch?"

What did she say to that? The man made her itchy. She shrugged. "If you want."

He chuckled and slid onto one of the stools at the island.

She sighed and measured rice into the dish. "Did you have a good afternoon?"

"I did."

"You sound surprised." She glanced over before unwrapping the chicken and starting to arrange it on top of the rice.

"Maybe I am. It's a little surreal to meet grandparents for the first time when you're twenty-six." He shrugged. "They're good people though. That's been obvious since I first started calling. It's kind of them to take me in. I'm sorry it makes more work for you."

She shook her head. "It doesn't. Not really. One more person to feed in the overall scheme isn't anything to worry about. It's good you came."

"You think?"

Maria stopped working and turned to study him. Why did he care what she thought? "I do. The Hewitts love your family. Your dad's treatment of them breaks their heart. When you started calling, you brought a little bit of joy that couldn't come from anywhere else. Your sister being here earlier this month? Even more. They love you."

"They don't know me."

"Doesn't matter. They love you all the same." She smiled and went back to fixing up the casserole. He might try to hide it, but there was hurt under the skin there. Maybe he didn't even realize it. He needed Jesus. If he stayed here long, it didn't seem likely he'd leave without Him. "Did you go see the horses?"

"Not yet. I was chatting with Betsy. Then Wayne came home. He said he'd take me around after supper."

"Make him wait until tomorrow when the sun's up. It's going to be cold tonight. You don't want to wander around in the dark and cold."

"You're right about that." Cyan grinned.

Those ridiculous flutters in her belly started up again. Her face edged into a scowl. Maria dumped cheese over the top of the concoction and carried it to the oven. "I'll be back in about an hour to finish up. There's a drawer with snacks in the fridge if you get munchy before then."

"Can I come?"

She frowned. "What? Why?"

"Betsy and Wayne drove into town. They said something about needing more Christmas lights." He shrugged. "I don't have anything else to do."

He should've gone with them. They would've loved to show him around Taos. And it would've kept him out of her hair. She sighed. "Yeah, all right. Come on. Any good at Chinese Checkers?"

"I don't know. I've never played."

Maria's jaw dropped. "How? That's practically unAmerican."

"Or unChinese?"

She snorted out a laugh. "Who knows if the game's even from China? All I know is Calvin loves it. I was going to see if he wanted to play while the food cooked."

Cyan looked up from swiping and tapping at his phone. "Says here the game was invented in Germany."

Maria laughed. "Of course it was. Well, you read the rules, I'll get the board and Calvin."

He nodded and followed behind her.

She forced herself to stop looking over her shoulder. He'd either come or he wouldn't. At the door to her cabin she took a deep breath. Other than Wayne, she'd never invited a man into their space. Her stomach twisted into knots. Maybe this was a mistake.

"You sure you don't want to play another round of checkers? Chinese or otherwise?" Cyan leaned back in one of the deep chairs in the living room of the main house.

Calvin was curled up on one end of the sofa, his eyes drooping. He shook his head.

Maria dried her hands on the dish towel and hung it on its hook before turning off the light in the kitchen and joining the rest of them. She ruffled Calvin's hair, pausing with her hand on his forehead. Still cool. Maybe it was a growth spurt.

"Dinner was delicious." Cyan smiled at Maria. "Thanks for including me."

"We're just so glad you're here. You'll stay for Christmas, won't you?" Wayne leaned forward and propped his elbows on his knees. "We can always use another hand at the bonfire."

"Bonfire?" Cyan frowned. "You have a Christmas bonfire?"

Betsy laughed. "Thursday through Sunday every weekend leading up to Christmas. There are sleigh rides and carol sings and crafts for the kids. It's one way we try to give back to the community, by giving them a little extra joy around the holidays. Plus, it's a chance to tell them about Jesus."

Cyan nodded.

Maria watched him for a moment before adding, "Some people come up to cut their trees, as well."

"Wait. Cut a tree? Like a real tree?" Cyan frowned. "Isn't that bad?"

Wayne shook his head. "Nope. The men have been out marking available trees for the last couple of weeks. We look for the ones that are too close to larger, more established trees. Cutting out the suckers helps the forest thrive. Maybe people don't get a perfectly shaped tree, but they get the satisfaction of having sawed it down themselves and a fun afternoon hiking with their family out of it."

"Calvin was already asking if we were still going Thursday." Maria rested her hand on her son's leg. He didn't brush it off like he normally would. She peeked closer. His eyes were nearly shut.

"That's the plan." Betsy winked. "There ought to be some perks for living on the ranch. First pick of the trees is one. Is he feeling okay?"

Maria sighed. "He says he is. But I think I'm going to take him home and make it an early night. Sorry."

"Don't be sorry." Cyan stood as Maria did. "Can I carry him for you?"

"Carry—no, he can walk. Calvin, come on, let's go."

Calvin tried to uncurl and stand, but sank back into the sofa.

Maria chewed her lower lip and glanced at Cyan. "You're sure you don't mind?"

"Not at all." He stooped and scooped the boy into his arms. "Come on, champ, let's get you home."

Maria glanced over her shoulder at Wayne and Betsy and held her hands together, mouthing the word *pray* at them. Something was wrong with her son, and she hadn't the faintest idea what it might be.

In the cabin, Maria gestured for Cyan to set Calvin down outside the bathroom door. "I can get it from here. I appreciate the help."

"Happy to do it." He tucked his hands in his pockets. "Let me know if there's more I can do?"

Maria gave a jerky nod and prodded Calvin in to use the toilet. "I'm sure he's fine. Just tired. Maybe growing or fighting off a cold."

She'd keep saying that to herself as long as she needed.

3

Cyan padded into the living room of his grandparents' home. It was still dark outside and everything was quiet. He'd always been an early riser. On the converted school bus with his parents and siblings where he had grown up, that was a distinct disadvantage. It had, at least, taught him to move quietly. He crossed to the floor-to-ceiling windows that made the back wall of the two-story room and peered outside. He could just make out the shapes of some of the cabins where Maria and the ranch hands lived. His lips curved. That would make an interesting band name.

Was one of the three men who worked for his grandparents involved in Maria's life? Not like it mattered, of course. He'd only just met her. Plus, she had a little boy. He shook his head. There was no point in lying to himself. He was interested in her. She was beautiful—that glossy black hair and her high cheekbones were arresting. Despite her initial prickliness, and continued guardedness, she was interesting to talk to. And *that* wasn't something he'd found in entirely too long.

Fat snowflakes fell from the sky and coated the ground. How much would they get? They were high enough up, they had to be used to getting absolutely dumped on, but he wasn't. Unlike the majority of his family, he didn't head south every winter, but he did tend to avoid places with lots of snow. There was no redeeming quality to snow. It was cold, wet, and it made everything slippery.

He sighed and turned, moving to settle in one of the chairs grouped around the fireplace. Cyan could probably figure out how to light a fire. He pictured cheery flames crackling and warming the room. How noisy would the process be though? Not worth the risk. Just because he was up when it was barely four thirty didn't mean his grandparents needed to be. If he woke them, they'd likely suggest he move to a spare cabin rather than the guest room he'd opted for when given a choice.

Cyan dug his cell out of the pocket of his pajama pants and opened his work email. Technically he was on vacation this week, but that never seemed to keep the missives from coming. It was always better to respond sooner than later. Even if it meant he didn't get a true vacation. It wasn't like he was in an office forty hours a week having the life drained out of him with small talk and time-wasting meetings. Not that he didn't attend his share of meetings, but the ability to mute them and do something else while his boss droned on was priceless.

"You're up early."

Cyan looked up as Wayne clicked on a table lamp and lowered himself into a chair. He looked like an older, softer version of Cyan's father. The blue eyes and slightly bulbous nose were identical, but where his father's chin was square with a sharp jaw line, Wayne's jaw curved some. Maybe it was the neatly trimmed beard that made the difference? Had his father ever had facial hair?

"Bad habit, sorry. Did I wake you?" Cyan frowned at the latest email and hit the phone's power button. He'd have to call his boss later.

"Not at all. I've been getting up early my whole life. Early to bed, early to rise." Wayne shrugged. "The animals always preferred it, though I don't think the boys are even up quite this soon. Betsy, now? She can sleep until noon, if you let her."

Cyan chuckled. He couldn't quite picture his bubbly grandmother as a late riser.

"You want some coffee?" Wayne glanced toward the kitchen. "Maria usually leaves the pot set up, so all I have to do is turn it on."

"I'll get it." Cyan stood and studied the older man for a moment. "I really appreciate you letting me stay."

Wayne grinned. "Boy, if you think you had a choice once you showed up here, you're kidding yourself. Betsy has her way, you'll never leave."

Never leave. Surprisingly, that didn't sound as awful as it probably should. Of his siblings, Cyan was probably the least inclined to wander. Well, after his sister Indigo. She'd settled down—married, even—two years ago and seemed to be thriving. That was why he didn't have some sort of tiny home, though. He preferred to house sit or, in a pinch, find a hotel with weekly rates. He wasn't opposed to settling down. He just hadn't found his place yet.

With the coffee brewing, he returned to the great room and his grandfather. "So what's a typical day for you?"

"It's different these days. Now that we've got Tommy, Morgan, and Joaquin handling the horses, I don't have much to do. Usually, I spend the first hour of the day with coffee and my Bible. After that, I try to take it as it comes. There's always something to do, even if it's just go for a walk with Betsy in the snow."

Cyan smiled. That was a nice mental image. "Don't let me keep you from your reading."

"You want to join me?"

Reading the Bible? Out of curiosity only, Cyan had downloaded the Bible app onto his phone after Azure had started talking about Christianity. There were all kinds of reading plans available. When he had time—or made time—he was working through one that was supposed to introduce him to Jesus. It was interesting. But some part of him held back, the raging tirades his father used to go on ringing in his memory. "Sure. I guess?"

Wayne smiled and started to lever himself up. "I'll get you a Bible."

"Got one." Cyan held up his phone. "Why don't I get some coffee for us, first? How do you take it?"

"Just black is fine, but if you need creamer there should be some in the fridge. And there's sugar in a bowl on the counter. Your grandmother likes hers all done up."

He was with his grandmother, then. He'd never understood people who could drink black coffee. The pot was still in the final stages of brewing, so Cyan opened cupboards until he found mugs and a spoon then went to collect the creamer and chuckled. Betsy must like flavored creamer, too. He grabbed the bottle of gingerbread latte creamer and sniffed it. Oh, yeah. And he wasn't going to need sugar after adding this.

With the coffee in hand, he shuffled back to his chair.

"Thanks." Wayne took a long sip and then sighed. "Nothing like that first taste, is there?"

Cyan drank from his own mug. Maybe he'd added a tad too much gingerbread, but it was still good. "Nope."

"So. You have a Bible on your phone. You reading it?"

Cyan lifted his shoulders and worked to ignore the itch that was forming between them. It was like being in college all over again, when the professors just seemed to know who was doing the work and who was coasting. "Some."

"Where'd you start?"

Was he supposed to remember? Cyan swiped on his phone and opened the app, then tapped the icon that took him to the plan he was working through. "Um. Mark? Now I'm in John."

Wayne nodded. "Learning anything?"

"I guess." How did he put it into words? "I like reading about the miracles they say Jesus did. He seems like a good guy who got a bad rap."

"But just a man?"

Cyan sighed. "I guess I'm tripping over that, a little. I mean, if Jesus was God—first you have to say, okay, there's a God, right? So then you have God and Jesus and the Spirit—is that three gods? Except it says they're one, and that's weird. And then why would God send Jesus here to be a man just so he could die? That seems stupid. He's God. He should just smite the people who don't believe. It's all kind of elaborate, isn't it? Why would God bother with wanting people to choose to believe? Just get rid of the ones who don't so people realize there's no point in not."

"You'd like to be forced into it, then? No choice?"

"Well, no. From here, at least, no. But if I didn't know any different, would it matter?"

Wayne laughed. "All right, I guess that's fair. Here's the thing. God didn't make people into worship robots. He didn't want that. He wanted a relationship. That doesn't come from force."

A relationship. With God. "Still kind of a lopsided relationship, isn't it? I mean, I like my boss well enough, but I know we can't really be friends—not true friends—because he's my boss. We're not equals."

"But your boss doesn't love you unconditionally, either. He's looking for something from you—customer satisfaction, a certain number of hours of work each day, that sort of thing. There's a reason we use family terms, like father, to refer to God. It's hard, sometimes, when our fathers let us down, to see that God is the one father who will never fail." Wayne looked away, staring into the unlit fireplace.

Father. Cyan loved his dad. Even mostly liked him. But he hadn't been excited about hanging around any longer than he absolutely had to. As soon as he'd graduated from high school, he'd been off that bus and on his own. He checked in with them now and then, but never really felt like they cared one way or the other.

"Keep reading, Cyan, with an open heart, if you can. I'd love nothing more than to see you find faith in Jesus." Wayne flipped open his Bible and started to read.

Cyan sipped his coffee and stared at his phone. Finally, he tapped the next suggested reading and his eyes traveled down the screen, stopping at the words that seemed to leap out at him. *For God so loved the world, that He gave his one and only son, that whosoever believes in him shall not perish but have eternal life.*

What kind of love must that take? He couldn't quite wrap his mind around it.

"Can I fix you something for breakfast?" Betsy glanced over from where she was filling her coffee cup in the kitchen. "Maria doesn't usually come over until after she gets Calvin on the school bus."

"The bus comes up here?" They weren't in the middle of nowhere, exactly, but the ranch was a ranch, which meant it wasn't in the center of town, either.

Betsy laughed. "Sure does. Picks him up at the top of the road, by the big sign. Several of the other places up this way have school-aged kids too. Food?"

"Sure. But only if you're fixing something for yourself. I can manage on my own."

"I know you can, but I didn't get the chance to spoil you when you were younger. Seems like the least I can do is make you some pancakes now."

"I won't say no to pancakes. Thanks. Can I help?"

Betsy shook her head. "Nope. But you can come sit up here at the bar and keep me company."

That was easy enough. Cyan stood and stretched before moving seats. Once Betsy was up, Wayne had left to shower. Had they agreed to give each other time alone with him? Was that for them or were they trying not to overwhelm him? Either way, it was sweet. He set his empty mug on the counter next to his phone and propped his chin in his hands.

"Can I get you a refill?"

"I've had two."

"Live on the edge, have a third." She reached for the mug and smiled. "I see creamer in there."

Heat warmed his cheeks. "I'm a sucker for the flavored ones."

"That's my boy." Betsy fixed him coffee and set it in front of him before crossing the kitchen to collect things out of the pantry. "So, what have you been up to this morning?"

"Checking some work email, talking with Wayne." He shrugged. It was easier—better—to keep it vague. He wasn't ready for another conversation about God right now.

"Work have anything interesting to say? Seems to me everyone would be on vacation this week if they could be."

"You'd think, right? My boss seems to only ever take off the week between Christmas and New Year's. So he's still shooting out messages left and right. I'm going to give him a call in a little bit. I think maybe he got something confused."

"Oh?" She measured flour into a bowl and glanced over at him, eyebrows lifted.

"Yeah." Cyan frowned and pulled up the email again. "He's saying they want me on site at one of our customers' main office in New York City starting in January."

"I've always wanted to visit New York City. It seems like it'd be a unique experience." She cracked an egg into the bowl and began to mix. "Why would that not be intended for you?"

"Lots of reasons. First is that he's talking six months to a year. He knows I don't do big cities except for short—one or two days max—visits. I can't seem to breathe when I'm there. Tried it, early on, and was sicker than I've ever been. Plus, the job I have is flexible work location. Six months to a year? That's practically permanent. I need to understand what he's trying to do." Cyan rubbed the back of his neck. He wasn't opposed to working on just one customer account if that was what they needed, but it wasn't going to be one in New York City.

"Then I guess it's a good idea to call. What if he says it wasn't misdirected? Will you go?" She tapped the whisk against the side of the bowl before setting it in the sink and reaching for one of the pans that hung on a rack above.

"I don't know. I'm kind of hoping I don't have to figure that out."

Betsy smiled. "Then I'll pray that you get clear direction."

He chuckled. "That's something Azure would say."

"Is it? I wish she could've stayed longer, but it sounded like she needed to get back to Virginia to straighten things out with her young man."

Cyan winced. He wasn't used to thinking of his sister having someone serious in her life. From their brief conversations and text, this Matt guy was pretty serious. "Yeah. I—"

The kitchen door flew open and slammed against the wall as Maria, wearing the same clothes she'd worn the day before, albeit considerably more rumpled, hurried in. Her hair looked like she'd combed fingers through it, barely, and there was a fuzzy haze of panic clinging to her. "Where's Wayne?"

"I don't know, dear. I can—"

Maria cut Betsy off, her gaze arrowing to Cyan. "Can you come? I need help getting Calvin into the car."

"Did he miss the bus?" Cyan set down his coffee and stood, tucking his phone into his pocket.

"No. Something's wrong. He's not getting out of bed. He was up and down all night in the bathroom. I'm taking him to urgent care. Maybe it's just a cold and they won't be able to do something, but I can't seem to let it go. So I'll suck up the co-pay for peace of mind."

"Let me get my coat. I'll come with you." Cyan glanced at Betsy. "Sorry about the pancakes."

"Don't you worry about that. I'll put the batter in the fridge and we'll have them later. You go with Maria."

"No. I just need—" Maria broke off at Betsy's glare and nodded. "Okay. Thank you."

Cyan hurried to the guest bedroom he was using. He shoved his feet into sneakers and grabbed his coat. It'd be better if he had boots—the snow was starting to stick to everything—but he could only do what he could do. Jogging back to the kitchen, he paused to kiss his grandmother's cheek before he nodded at Maria. "Lead the way."

Her gaze flitted to his shoes. "Your feet are going to get wet."

He shrugged. "I've had worse. I'll be okay."

"All right. Thanks." Maria twisted her fingers together as she hurried between the main house and her cabin. "He's usually bouncy. Hops out of bed talking a million miles an hour and races me to the bus stop. That's been easing off some, lately, but I figured maybe it was because he was finally listening when I told him I needed time to wake up. But now...what if I've missed something?"

"I'm sure he'll be fine." Cyan wasn't sure of that at all, but it seemed like the right thing to say. He glanced at the kitchen on his way through to the bedrooms, noting the plate set out with eggs and toast. He smiled a little. Must be nice to wake up to that every morning. His mother had never been one for breakfast. If anything, they'd had a box of cereal shoved at them, but usually it was a vague hand gesture toward where the food was kept.

Calvin lay in the top bunk of rustic wooden bunk beds, wearing fuzzy pajamas that had space ships all over them. "I'm coming, Mom."

"Oh, honey. Can you sit up so Mr. Hewitt can get you down?"

"Hey, buddy, ready for another ride?" Cyan reached up and awkwardly helped Calvin wiggle to the ladder where he could be scooped up without the rail getting in the way. "Up we go."

"Gotta pee."

Cyan chuckled. "We'll make a pit stop on the way. You want to grab some socks and shoes so his feet don't get cold?"

Maria nodded.

Cyan carried the boy into the hall and set him down gently by the bathroom. "Got it?"

"Yeah." He took a couple of stumbling, shuffling steps into the small room.

Cyan turned away and studied the photos of Calvin—sometimes with Maria, but more often with a horse—hanging in the hallway.

"Can you make it to the couch, baby?" Maria's voice was close.

Cyan turned.

Calvin blinked, frowning, and rubbed his eyes. "Yeah. I'm okay, Mom."

"Uh huh. Let's get socks and shoes on and go from there." She turned, her lower lip caught between her teeth. "Maybe I don't need—"

"Let me help you. Please? Even if he can get around on his own, I'd like to know I was there if you did need me." Cyan had probably never uttered more heartfelt words. The question was why, when he'd known someone for so short a time, did he feel that way? He wasn't prone to the need to rescue damsels. In fact, generally, he believed women were more than capable of slaying whatever dragons got in their way all on their own. But something about Maria and her son tugged at him. So he was going to see it through, if she'd let him.

Her voice was grudging. "Yeah. All right."

He followed her down the short hallway, trying not to notice—or at least not focus on—the snug fit of her jeans. It was entirely inappropriate. And entirely too eye catching.

Calvin sat on the couch slowly dragging socks over his feet. His face was pulled down into a pout. "I don't wanna go to the doctor."

Maria smiled and handed him a boot. "I don't blame you. We're still going."

"I'm gonna miss the party at school. Sancho said his mom was bringing cupcakes."

"We'll make cupcakes this weekend, okay? Or maybe the first batch of Christmas cookies? You can try out the rocket shaped cookie cutters we got last year."

Calvin frowned.

"Do you put sprinkles on them?" Cyan perched on the arm of the couch and tried to catch Calvin's eyes. "Or that sugar that has the big crystals so it's crunchy on top?"

Calvin nodded. "I like that kind."

"It's even better if you frost the cookie first and *then* add the sugar."

"Yeah?" Calvin got his second boot on and looked at his mom. "Can we do that?"

"I'll have to see if we have enough powdered sugar to make icing. Maybe after the doctor, we can swing by the store and get another bag just to be sure. Come on now, up and let's get your coat on."

Between Cyan and Maria, they got Calvin out the door and buckled in the back seat of Maria's car.

"You really don't have to come."

"I know. I want to." Cyan tugged open the passenger door and climbed in.

"Suit yourself." Maria sighed and got behind the wheel. She glanced into the rearview mirror and frowned.

Cyan turned to look. Calvin appeared to have fallen back asleep.

4

Maria prayed under her breath the whole way into town. They weren't all for Calvin, the snow was making the roads slick and some of the turns on the hill were iffy. The road crews were clearly hard at work, but these conditions always made her a little nervous. The man sitting in the passenger seat wasn't helping that situation. He was too handsome for his own good with that slightly too-long brown hair that curled over his collar and the gray eyes that seemed to look directly into her soul.

Fishtailing slightly, she turned into the parking lot of the urgent care and parked. She looked into the backseat and frowned. "Calvin, honey? Wake up."

"Why don't I just carry him?" Cyan hit the button on his seatbelt and pushed open the car door. "I suspect that'll wake him, but it's easier than getting him to walk."

"Okay. Thank you. Again."

A hint of dimples flashed as he smiled. "You've gotta stop saying that. It's my privilege."

Privilege? Maria barely managed not to snort. If he felt honored to help carry a sick kid to urgent care, he needed to get a life. When all the car doors were shut, she hit the lock button on her key fob and picked her way across the semi-cleared sidewalk to the main door. She held it open while Cyan angled Calvin through.

They had the heat up way too high. Doctors always seemed to do that, as if people were going to be coming in wearing shorts and T-shirts while it was snowing outside. Sweat beaded on Maria's back as she walked to the reception desk and explained the problem.

Carrying a clipboard with forms, she headed to the seats Cyan and Calvin had staked out. There were three other people in the waiting area. Hopefully this wouldn't take too long. She could appease her overactive mom-worrying-gene and get back to the ranch. There was a lot of prep for Thanksgiving that needed to be done still. And after that, Christmas was going to be in full swing. With all the new snow, it wouldn't surprise her if Wayne wanted to get the sleigh out for their trip into the forest for Christmas trees on Friday.

She glanced over at Cyan as she reached the bottom of the first form and frowned. "What's that?"

Cyan tilted his phone away from Calvin. "It's a little strategy game. Think Risk with aliens. Is that okay? I should've asked. Sorry."

She eyed the screen. He was right, he should've asked. Generally, she tried to keep video games to a bare minimum. They couldn't afford the gaming console Calvin desperately wanted. Even if they could, she wasn't sold on him getting online with friends to shoot aliens. Shooting anything seemed like a bad idea for a kid his age. Except, of course, that Tommy and Morgan generally took Calvin out to fire .22s with them at least twice over summer break. So it wasn't as if he didn't understand guns. She sighed. "Seems okay. No language?"

Cyan shook his head. "Nothing but music. And captions. But the words just say who's attacking who. No trash talk."

"All right. Thanks." She flipped the form over and paused to dig in her purse for her insurance card. Not that insurance would pay for the visit. Wayne and Betsy offered as many insurance options as they could, but the pickings were slim. High deductibles were the name of the game. That and prayer. Lots and lots of prayer that no one got seriously ill. Her gaze darted to her son, who was tapping raptly at Cyan's phone, seeming almost normal. Was this a big waste of time and money?

Cyan leaned closer, his voice low. "You okay?"

"Yeah. Of course." No need to bother him with the worries of where any of the money was going to come from. She hurried through the rest of the forms and walked them back up to the desk.

A nurse poked her head through the door that opened into the waiting area. "Calvin?"

Maria frowned slightly but stood. Shouldn't they have taken people in the order they got there? She glanced over at the others in the waiting room and offered an apologetic smile. "Come on, Cal."

"Can I bring your phone?" Calvin gave Cyan a hopeful look.

"If your mom says it's okay, sure." Cyan glanced at Maria.

"You don't mind?"

Cyan shook his head.

"Okay. Thank you."

Cyan just grinned.

Maria took Calvin's hand. "We shouldn't be long."

"It's not a big deal. I'm fine." As if to prove his point, he scooted down in his seat and stretched his legs out in front of him.

She needed to stop worrying about Cyan and focus on her son. Except, of course, thinking about Cyan kept her mind off the possibilities of what could be wrong. That and the man was mouthwatering. Not that she was looking. Much.

"Right this way." The nurse, whose nametag proclaimed her "Lucy," gestured to a doorway on their left that had a curtain hanging halfway across it. "We'll go in here and get some vitals. Any fever?"

Calvin turned and looked at Maria.

"No." Maria fought not to sigh. Calvin was terrible about speaking to adults, always looking to her to do it for him. She didn't usually force the issue.

"Okay. Have a seat." When Calvin was settled, Lucy slipped a thermometer under Calvin's tongue, wrapped his arm in a kid-sized blood pressure cuff, and clipped an oxygen monitor to his index finger. "Stay still, okay?"

Calvin gave a tiny nod.

Lucy looked at Maria. "Date of birth?"

Maria rattled it off.

Lucy consulted her tablet and tapped the screen. "It says here he's been off—more tired than usual, edging on lethargic. Any other symptoms?"

Were there? He'd been drinking more, but the air was always dry in the winter. She'd been drinking more, too. "I don't think so. It's just—something in my gut said he needed to be seen."

"You look up his symptoms online?" The nurse gave a small smile.

Maria's cheeks heated. "I wasn't going to, but then I couldn't sleep and..."

"One thing led to another. Sure. What did you come up with?" Lucy took the thermometer out of Calvin's mouth and tapped the tablet. "Temp's normal, BP and O2 look good. Hop on the scale over here, okay?"

"Nothing specific. One article said to ask about blood sugar, but there's no history of diabetes in our family." That she knew of. It's not like she'd done a thorough medical workup of the one night stand that resulted in her son. But *he* wasn't a diabetic, so really, what were the odds? She glanced at the large numbers on the scale and bit her lip. Had he lost weight?

The nurse noted Calvin's weight and pointed across the hall to an exam room. "Go on in over there. Has he been drinking more? Having to use the bathroom more often?"

Maria nodded. "I thought with winter—drier air—it's not really much more than usual."

"Okay. Get settled. The doctor should be with you soon."

Maria and Calvin crossed the hall into the exam room. Calvin crawled up on the table and sagged back, curling his legs up, and swiping listlessly at Cyan's phone.

She studied her baby, her heart constricting.

Someone knocked.

"Come in." That was fast. Urgent care never seemed to embody the term urgent in Maria's experience. At this rate, they'd be out of here in time for Calvin to make a little bit of his school day.

"Just me." Lucy came in with a clear plastic cup and a small rectangular machine. She looked at Calvin and smiled. "Think you could go to the bathroom for me?"

He nodded.

"Okay. I'll show you where in a second. First, I want to check your blood sugar, then we can maybe put your mom's mind at ease after her late night web searching." Lucy winked at Calvin. "It'll be a little prick on your finger, okay?"

He nodded again.

"See? Easy. You don't even really need a bandage. Come this way, and I'll show you the bathroom. You can wait here, Mom. I'll make sure he gets back when he's finished."

"Okay." Maria fidgeted and finally stood up, peering out the door to watch Calvin and the nurse navigate the short distance to the bathroom. She waited in the doorway, offering a weak smile when Lucy spied her watching. It wasn't wrong to be protective. Especially when her child was sick.

Calvin was back in the hallway offering Lucy the plastic cup before shuffling back to the exam room. He threw his arms around Maria and buried his face in her side.

Maria stooped and scooped him up, staggering a little before settling on one of the chairs. She kissed his head and rocked slightly from side to side as nerves gnawed in her stomach.

There was a brisk knock and a stern-looking woman strode in. "Mrs. Sanchez?"

Maria nodded. It was never worth explaining that it should be Miss. In the overall scheme of things, it didn't matter. Let them assume she was married.

"Would you like us to get your husband?"

"My husba—oh, Cyan? He's just a friend. I'm not married."

The woman nodded. "We've called an ambulance. Your son needs to be admitted and evaluated immediately. His blood sugar is over 400. We haven't tested the urine yet, but it's very likely with that reading that he has diabetic ketoacidosis. That can be very bad. On the positive side, you brought him in and from the symptoms you've described we've caught it quickly."

Maria's arms tightened around Calvin as she tried to absorb the doctor's words. "I have my car. Would it be faster to drive him?"

"No. We paged the on-call when we called for transport, hopefully they'll have instructions to start treatment on the ride." The doctor cocked her head to the side. "Let me go get your friend. Maybe he can drive your car over and meet you there. Cyan, you said?"

Maria nodded, her brain still scrambling to catch up. Diabetes. She'd read about it the night before. It wasn't something that got fixed. It was permanent. She closed her eyes as they filled with tears. She couldn't break down now. Now yet. Right now, Calvin needed her.

"Hey."

Maria blinked rapidly before turning to see Cyan hovering uncomfortably in the door.

"They said you wanted to see me?"

She cleared her throat. "They're sending us to the hospital."

"Oh. That doesn't sound good." He frowned. "Do you want me to drive?"

"No, it's not that. An ambulance is coming." This time a tear worked its way out and slipped down her cheek. Maria ignored it. "Maybe you could take the car back up to the ranch? I don't know when we'll be able to come home."

"Do you have your cell phone?"

"Of course."

"Where?"

What did that matter? She nodded to her purse on the seat beside her.

Cyan reached into the bag and drew out her phone. He pushed the button. "What's the code?"

Huffing out a breath, she unlocked it for him, jostling Calvin a little to be able to see what she was doing. "Why?"

He tapped at the screen and handed it back. "Because now you have my number, and I have yours. If I can find my phone?"

"On the bed."

Cyan turned and grabbed it. "Thanks. Want me to wait until the ambulance gets here? Or I can follow you to the hospital. I don't want to leave you alone."

"I'm not alone. God's got this. He's got us. We're okay. Would you tell Betsy and Wayne?"

"Of course. You know they're going to want to visit."

She closed her eyes and nodded. He was right. And Thanksgiving. What was going to happen to the food she was supposed to be prepping? "You know what? I'll call them when we get there and I know what's going on."

He studied for several heartbeats before blowing out a breath. "All right. Did they say what's wrong?"

"Diabetes." Her stomach sank. Saying it out loud made it seem so real. This wasn't any part of the plans she had for their future.

What was she supposed to do?

5

Cyan waited until he'd navigated the unfamiliar roads back to the ranch and caught Wayne and Betsy up on the situation before excusing himself to call his boss. That hadn't gone well. All in all, it was shaping up to be a rather horrible day and it wasn't quite lunch time.

He didn't *want* to be on site in New York City. Cities in general gave him claustrophobia. But New York? He'd been once—to visit this same customer, in fact—and had sworn he'd never go back. He should've done a worse job on that visit, though, because they'd asked for him by name. Oh, sure, they'd said if he was available, but his boss's theory was that a good contractor made sure whatever the client asked for was provided. Right now, that was Cyan. At least they'd given him until after New Year's.

Running a hand through his hair—the hair he'd meant to get cut before showing up at his grandparents' house—he sank to the edge of the bed. His cell buzzed, and Cyan groaned before checking the readout. The dread that was pooling in his gut dissipated when he saw it was his younger sister, Skye.

"Hey."

"Yo." Skye's voice always made Cyan smile. "Heard through the grapevine that you're at dad's parents'. How's that going?"

"The grapevine? That would be Azure, I imagine?"

"Mom, actually. But I think she got it from Azure. So?"

"So, what?"

"Come on, bro. What are they like?"

"They're great. Just about what you'd expect. Maybe not in looks—although Wayne is like a forecast of Dad in twenty years."

"Which means you in what, forty?"

"Har. Har. I'm not a carbon copy of Dad."

"Keep telling yourself that. What about grandma?"

"Betsy? She's not plump and snuggly, but she's still warm and welcoming."

Skye snickered. "Plump and snuggly? What were you thinking you'd find? Mrs. Claus?"

Heat crawled up Cyan's neck. His mental picture *had* been a lot like that. "Yeah, well, how was I supposed to know? It's not like we've had grandparents before."

"But we've known people who were grandparents. They're just people with kids who had kids."

"Whatever." Cyan frowned. His youngest sibling was good at giving him a hard time. Too good. "Anyway, I like them. A lot. And the ranch is great, too. It's like a slice of paradise."

"I thought you were in New Mexico."

"I am."

"Paradise is tropical, man. Preferably with a rainforest nearby."

Cyan laughed. "Maybe for you. For me? It's here. I'm gonna hate leaving in January."

"Already making plans to go?"

"Only because of work. Apparently they need me in New York for one of our biggest clients. I'm trying to wiggle out of it, but so far no dice."

"New York? Not City, right, just somewhere else in the state?"

"I wish. Manhattan."

"Cy, man, get out of it. Do you not remember how crazy you were when you went there last time? How long was that? A week?"

"Yeah, I know. But all my boss hears is that I don't care for it." He lacked the words to explain the tightness that pervaded every pore the longer he was there. "Maybe it'll be better this time."

"Good luck with that. On the flip side, maybe you can stop in Virginia and meet this Matt guy Azure's in love with."

"In love? You sure?"

"According to Mom. For Az to be putting down roots, it has to be serious. She was always the most resistant to that."

"True. Then there's you. Where are you now?"

"Yeah, yeah. At least my travel is all for my job. I do have an apartment."

"Right. How many days have you lived there this year?"

Skye sighed. "Not enough. I'm working on it. With Mom and Dad settling in Arizona, it's kind of like it gave us all permission, you know? I'm not sure any of us were as in love with the wandering life as we let on."

Cyan shrugged. He didn't hate it. He didn't love it, either, but it was what he was used to. Even if he had a base of operations, his job did ask him to travel a good bit. He wouldn't be as bad as Skye, but travel was frequent enough that the flexibility of his living arrangements had always been a checkmark in the plus column. "I could settle here, easy."

"You think the grandparents would let you?"

"I think I'm going to ask and find out." The words startled him as they left his mouth. He hadn't planned to say anything of the sort. And yet, this could easily be home. He'd met the three ranch hands, Tommy, Joaquin, and Morgan, at lunch yesterday. From what he understood, they each had their own space. As did Maria. His heart clenched a little and he glanced at the clock on the nightstand. Still too early, probably, to check in with her and see how she was doing. They'd offered him one of the empty cabins. Was it possible that could be permanent? Just as soon as he was done talking to Skye, he was going to go ask Betsy.

"Good for you. Think you'll settle down, start a family?"

"Where'd that come from?" Cyan dragged his thoughts away from the picture of Maria that started to form. Sure, she was pretty. And nice. And Calvin was a delight. But that was a far cry from even asking her out.

"Dunno. Just figured you'd be next, after Azure."

"Indigo beat us all."

Skye laughed. "That's true. She always did her own thing, didn't she?"

"Pretty much from day one."

"Hey, I gotta run. But maybe if you're still around in the new year, I'll swing down and you can introduce me to the grandparents?"

"You can come even if I'm not here. I'll text you their phone number—they still have a land line, though Betsy texts on her cell, too. Give them a call and get to know them."

"Yeah? Okay. Don't be a stranger, Cy."

Cyan chuckled. "You either. Thanks for calling."

Tucking his cell in his pocket, Cyan headed toward the living room. He was going to ask about a cabin now. Before he chickened out.

"Cyan, honey?" Betsy came into the living room from the kitchen, phone in her hand. "Maria just texted me. Are you willing to take a bag down to the hospital for her? They're going to keep Calvin a couple of days. With Thanksgiving on Thursday, she's thinking probably Friday before they get home."

"Of course. You don't want to go? So you can see her?" Not that he didn't want to see Maria. Time had ticked extra slowly this afternoon as he played Chinese checkers with Wayne while waiting for Maria to get in touch with someone.

"I'd just as soon not. I know they handle the roads fine, but Wayne and I are getting to an age where we try not to venture out in the snow if we can help it."

That made sense. Sort of. They weren't *that* old. Maybe sixty? Sixty-five, tops? Both of them still got around like they were a lot younger. "She gave you a list?"

Betsy nodded. "I can go pack it all up. Tommy and Morgan got the paths cleared just after lunch and there hasn't been a ton more snow since then. I think we only ended up with six or seven inches. Once you get down the hill, you'll probably find it's stopped altogether. Give me ten, fifteen minutes?"

"No rush on my end." He glanced at Wayne. "Probably not enough time for you to beat me soundly again though."

Wayne chuckled. "I still can't believe your father never introduced you to this game. It was his favorite growing up."

Cyan sighed. There were, apparently, a lot of favorites of his dad's that had been thoroughly abandoned when he left home. "I'm sorry."

"Don't be. If anyone should be sorry, it's me. I feel like I chased him off." Wayne shook his head. "Parenting isn't for the faint of heart."

"Dad used to say that a lot."

"Did he?" Wayne laughed. "Well, there you go. At least he heard something I said. I'm glad you've come, Cyan, and I'm looking forward to getting to know you the longer you're here. Would you consider staying in the house through the holidays? If you want your own space sooner, I understand—the cabin's yours whenever, but it sure would be nice to have you in the main house for a bit."

"If you're sure, I'd like that." There was something nice about having other people around. He'd been on his own long enough that he'd grown used to it, but he wasn't in a hurry to get back to it.

"Excellent." Wayne sighed. "Then we'll plan to get you settled after Christmas so you have a little time to get organized before they ship you off to the city."

"Or we can wait until I get back. If you need the space for something?" It had been a bit of a revelation to find out there were close to a dozen currently empty cabins on the property. Some were only set up for summer camps—no kitchens, just bunk space. Those were out on the property a ways where, apparently, there was a larger lodge-type thing that handled meals for campers as well. Churches and community groups used the spaces and the hiking trails on the property from June through August. The place was in high demand, and the fees they charged, though reasonable, paid for the bulk of the year-round operation.

"Oh, no. Your cabin isn't one of the camp spaces. Maybe I wasn't clear. This used to be a cattle operation. That required quite a few more resident ranch hands than our current scope. So, we have living spaces for ten. We can go take a look at them tomorrow and you can make your choice."

"I'd like that. Wouldn't mind getting the two dollar tour of the place, actually."

"Didn't we—no, I guess we didn't, did we? With all the chaos this morning for Maria." Wayne shook his head. "Poor girl. That boy is the light of her life. I'm grateful it's something that can be managed, though. Not that it won't be a long road, but you can live a long, full life with diabetes if you take care of yourself."

Before Cyan could decide how to respond, Betsy bustled back in with two full duffel bags. "I threw in more than she asked for, but it's the hospital. They're both going to get tired of daytime television before half a day is up. So this one is mostly books and games, and I snuck in Maria's laptop and Calvin's tablet."

"Charging cords too?"

Betsy grinned at Cyan. "Yep. I've made that mistake and learned the hard way. Now you go on down, and don't rush back on our account. I suspect Maria could use a friend."

She probably could, which was why Cyan still didn't completely understand why he was the one going. Wayne and Betsy were practically family. "You could come down, too. I'd still be happy to drive."

There was a gleam in her eye as Betsy shook her head. "We'll go tomorrow."

Blowing out a breath, Cyan took the two bags. They were heavy. His grandmother had some serious muscle. She'd toted them so easily he'd assumed they'd be easy to carry. "Can I pick anything up for you in town before I come home?"

"If I think of something, I'll text you."

Cyan chuckled and gave a little wave. If she wasn't careful, Betsy was going to end up a texting addict. As he left the room, Wayne said something to Betsy that Cyan couldn't quite catch. But he did hear Betsy's joy-filled laugh. Whatever the joke was, it must've been a good one. That gleam in her eye though—he just hoped the joke didn't involve him.

Cyan tapped on the hospital room door and peeked in when he thought he heard someone speak.

Maria's eyebrows drew together and she stood. "Cyan? I thought Wayne or Betsy—or maybe both of them—would come down."

"I tried to talk them into it. I know I'm not who you want to see right now."

"Oh. No. That's not what I meant." She turned to look at Calvin who lay in the bed hooked up to IVs and a quietly beeping machine. "I just need to talk to them. Get their opinions on something."

Should he offer to help? Could he even help? She barely knew him. She certainly didn't care that she and her son tugged at a part of his heart he hadn't known existed. Now that he was going to be based at the ranch, he'd have time to get to know her properly and then, maybe she'd see the same things in him that he saw in her. For now? Maybe it was better to deliver the bags and go. "I've been told I'm a good listener."

She offered a sad smile. "I'm sure you are. It's just—"

"No, it's okay. I'm sorry. I don't know why I said that. You don't know me. Look, tell me where to put these and I'll get out of your hair." He hefted one of the duffels higher, jostling the gift bag that held an enormous stuffed dinosaur and a couple of puzzles he'd seen in the gift shop on the way in.

"Anywhere is fine." She stood and reached for the bags and her fingers brushed his. Did she not feel the electricity zipping between them?

Cyan set down the other duffel, still holding the gift bag. "This is from me. For Calvin. I noticed he had a lot of dinosaur stuff in his room. Thought maybe a little more wouldn't be a bad idea. Um. I left the receipt in there though. If it's too much, they said they'd take it back and I guess you could get a lifetime supply of get well cards or something instead."

Maria chuckled. "Dinosaurs are his favorite. It was sweet of you. Thanks."

"Sure." He put the gift bag on the floor next to the others and tucked his hands in his pockets. "Okay. Then I guess I'll go. Do you want me to have Betsy call you? You could ask your questions that way. Which of course you already knew. I'm leaving. Except—were you going to eat dinner?"

"They'll bring a tray up for Calvin. I think." She rubbed her hands over her face. "They're working to get his blood sugar stabilized, so maybe not. Food raises blood sugar, and we sure don't need that happening. I hadn't thought about it."

"Can I buy you a sandwich in the cafeteria? Calvin's resting. We could let the nurse know to call you if he wakes up.

It won't do you any good to starve. You need to be able to think clearly. I know for me, food helps with that."

"I can't leave him." Her fingers curled around the bar at the foot of the hospital bed. "I can't take that chance."

Cyan nodded. Of course not. Because she was a good mom. "Let me run down and get something then. I'll bring it back up."

"You don't mind?"

He shook his head. "Is it okay if I eat with you?"

She wrinkled her nose. "Food's better at home, but if you want to, I won't say no. I could use a friendly face."

Cyan grinned. "I'll be right back."

6

Maria watched Cyan go before sinking back into the recliner beside Calvin's bed. Her thoughts swirled, unfocused. Why had he come? Oh, sure, he'd said Betsy and Wayne hadn't wanted to risk the roads, but they drove in the snow all the time. Had he talked them out of it? Or had that been their excuse?

Betsy was constantly trying to get Maria to date. When Maria had made it clear none of the three ranch hands interested her, Betsy had even gone so far as to suggest online dating. And okay, fine, Maria appreciated the thought, but she was content. She had Calvin and a job she was good at. Maybe it wasn't what she'd dreamed of, but she was working toward that, too. Slowly. The equine therapy lessons they'd started at the ranch had been her idea. And even if she wasn't able to be completely in charge of them yet, she was assisting and getting practical experience. If she ever finished her online degree, she'd be able to work with their current occupational therapist and the program could expand.

She glanced over at Calvin. She'd planned to start two new courses in January. Now? It looked like she'd be deferring for the semester. There was no way she'd have the mental resources to learn how to help him manage this disease, keep up with her job, *and* increase her school workload. Thankfully, the fall semester class she was taking ended in three weeks and she was maintaining a solid A. Even if she wasn't able to finish her final paper, she should be able to squeak out a passing grade.

Cyan came back carrying two trays. He was tall and lanky and that mix of nerdy and buff that was absolutely her type. Something Betsy knew all too well. If her employer was matchmaking, she could have done a lot worse. But the timing was simply all wrong.

"The selection was every bit as awful as you'd imagine. So you have your choice of chicken salad or some sort of pseudo-Italian deli meat. I thought about the beef stroganoff, but it sort of embodied the word *congealed* and I couldn't bring myself to try it. These at least came with a bag of chips, so we know something will be edible."

Maria snickered. He could make her smile entirely too easily. "I'll take the chicken salad. Thanks. I appreciate this. And everything you did for us this morning."

He shrugged and perched on the cushion that ran the length of the room on what they laughingly called a window seat. They'd told Maria she could stretch out and sleep on it as well, but she planned to take her chances with the chair. It reclined enough that it had to be more comfortable. "Calvin's a cool kid. I'm happy to do it."

Was it just because of Calvin? Her heart sank. She chastised herself. What did it matter? Just because Betsy was matchmaking and Cyan was interesting and attractive didn't mean Maria was interested. Couldn't. Wouldn't. After all, he wasn't a believer and that was a mistake she wasn't making a second time. "Thank you, just the same."

He nodded and took a bite of his sub. "Well. It's not dreadful."

"That doesn't bode well." Maria sniffed her own food before shrugging and taking her bite. Fuel was fuel, and Cyan had been right, she needed to take care of herself so she could take care of her son.

"Can I ask you something?"

Maria lifted an eyebrow and nodded. "I'm not promising to answer."

"Sure. That's fine. I just wondered how, with something like this, you still believe that God is good." He frowned and opened his bag of corn chips. "I mean, Calvin's great. He's just a kid. He doesn't deserve this."

"No. You're right, he doesn't. That's life though, isn't it? We don't always get what we deserve, good or bad. I'm grateful for it. If we got what we deserved, God would never have sent Jesus to die for our sin." Maria sighed. "I've always seen it as a choice. You either choose to believe that God is good and that He has good things for us, or you don't."

"And diabetes is good?"

"It doesn't feel like it right now, no. But God can make something beautiful out of it. I believe that. I have to. So I trust God to do that. Maybe I'll never know what that is, but I know He's got this under control, even though it seems pretty hopeless right now."

"Hopeless? I thought the prognosis was good?"

Maria winced. "It is. I'm sorry. It's just long term—they'd like to get him set up with an insulin pump. It's a better way to manage the disease, especially since the new ones have a built in continuous glucose monitor so we'll have a better feel for his blood sugar all the time. And it's fewer finger pricks and syringes."

Cyan nodded.

"But my insurance doesn't cover it. They'll handle the regular supplies, but not the technology." Her eyes filled and she looked up at the ceiling while she took a deep breath. "He's seven. I just don't...three or four injections a day along with finger pricks to test his sugar? I want better for him than that. And I don't know what to do."

"That's what you wanted to talk to Wayne and Betsy about."

She managed a small nod and forced herself to take another bite of her dry, tasteless sandwich. "God's got this. I just don't know how yet."

"You're an incredible woman, do you know that?"

A tear spilled over onto her cheek as she laughed. "No."

"Well, you should." He crumpled his empty chip bag and stood. "I'll get out of your hair and tell Betsy you need to talk when I get back home. You have my number if you need anything. Anything. I'm serious."

"Sure." She set aside her tray and stood. "Thanks for dinner."

"Make sure you eat it."

Maria nodded, though she had no intention of choking anything else down. When he was gone, she sank back into her seat and sighed. The tears streamed down her cheeks. What had she been thinking, bringing up the insurance snag? It was no wonder he'd run away as fast as he could. She wasn't positive she'd done a very good job explaining her faith, either, and that gnawed at her. Cyan seemed to be so close to believing, but if he was one of those people who needed every answer thoroughly explained before he'd make that leap? Well, that didn't seem to be how God worked. At least not in her life.

She closed her eyes, leaned on the railing of Calvin's bed, and returned to pouring her heart out to her Heavenly Father.

"Welcome home!" Betsy opened her arms wide and grinned as Maria pushed open the passenger door of Cyan's car.

"Thanks. It's good to be out of the hospital. I'm sorry about Thanksgiving."

"Pfft." Betsy waved off the words. "We'll have our big meal tomorrow and no one will care one way or the other."

"Tomorrow. But the trees and the bonfires? Don't they start tonight?" Maria tugged open Calvin's door and brushed a hand over his hair as he stepped out of the car.

"We put it off a week. No one minds. It's more important that you two get settled." Betsy closed the distance between them and gave Maria a quick hug before pulling Calvin to her side. "You scared us, young man."

"Sorry, Mrs. Hewitt."

Betsy laughed. "Oh, hon. You know I'm teasing you. I'm just glad you're better."

Better? Maria shook her head. There was no "better" in store for him. Not yet. Maybe not ever. Still, his blood sugar was stable and they were learning the ups and downs of the disease and its treatment, even if it tied her stomach in knots to give him a shot full of insulin. She'd never had dreams of being a nurse. But she could do this. With God's help, the two of them would be fine. Her gaze darted over to Cyan, who hovered in the periphery with their bags. She gave herself a firm mental shake. She had no business thinking about a man like she thought about him. Especially not a man who wasn't a believer. *Yet.*

He was so close.

She was praying for Cyan almost as much as she prayed for Calvin now. Was that fair to her son? It wasn't as though she had a finite number of prayers she could use. Even if sometimes it seemed like she had a finite amount of time to spend talking with Jesus, she could still pray for both of them. Of course she could. This was just one more reason it was ridiculous to let this man get close to her.

Even if he did make her pulse flutter.

"All right, kiddo, let's go get our stuff put away. Mom's got laundry to start, and then I should spend some time in the kitchen prepping for our big meal tomorrow. You want to go see the horses?"

He brightened. "Can I?"

"I don't see why not." His blood sugar had been a happy one hundred ten at the hospital when they checked out. It shouldn't have been a long enough drive for that to have changed. Maria took a deep breath. She had to learn to trust God to handle it. He'd be going back to school on Monday. "Go on, buddy. I'll see you in a while, okay?"

Calvin let out a whoop.

"Hey, Cal, mind if I tag along? I haven't been to meet the horses yet." Cyan glanced over at Maria. "That okay?"

She nodded. Could he possibly understand how much it helped to know an adult was there and paying attention? It was likely that one of the guys would be in the stables, but they'd have work.

"Yeah. Come on, Cyan."

"Mr. Hewitt." Maria's correction was automatic. She reached for the bags. "I can take these."

"Is Mr. Cyan okay? Mr. Hewitt is going to get confusing with Wayne having the same last name." Cyan held the handles of the bags, refusing to let go.

"I guess. I just want him to be respectful of adults."

Cyan nodded. "I get that. Thus the Mr." He pointed a finger at Calvin. "Let's help your mom get these bags to the cabin first, okay? Then you can introduce me to the horses."

Calvin frowned but nodded and reached for his backpack, hefting it over his shoulder. "Let's hurry. Maybe we can find Mr. Morgan and he can get us an apple to feed them."

"I'm sure they'd like that." Maria ruffled Calvin's hair and started toward the cabin.

Betsy fell into step beside her while Calvin and Cyan were a few steps behind.

"Well now, that's nice to see."

Maria frowned at Betsy. "What?"

"My grandson. You." Betsy arched her eyebrows.

Maria shook her head. "He's just being nice."

"Mmm. I wouldn't be so sure." Betsy glanced over her shoulder then back at Maria. "He's had some good conversations with Wayne about Jesus, if that's what's worrying you."

How was she even supposed to respond to that? Of course that worried her. But it wasn't the only thing. She'd known Cyan less than a week. For that matter, how long had Wayne and Betsy actually known him? What did they know about him beyond that he was their grandchild? Everything in her heart said Cyan was a good, honorable man, and that if he knew Jesus he'd be exactly what she was looking for. But her head reminded her that appearances weren't always what they seemed. She had only to look as far as Calvin's father to have proof of that.

Maybe it was better to stay quiet.

They arrived at her cabin and Maria gestured to a spot just inside the door. "Just drop everything there. I can get it from here. Thanks. Go see the horses."

"Don't stay too long though, Mr. Hewitt still wants to get the sleigh hooked up so we can get a tree for the main house. And yours, if you're ready for it, Maria? No rush, of course." Betsy smiled.

"Can we, Mom? Please?" Calvin clasped his hands under his chin and sent her a pleading look.

Maria sighed. A Christmas tree was the last thing on her mind right now. There was laundry to do, diabetic supplies to figure out how and where to store, and a thousand things at the main house for the postponed Thanksgiving meal to handle. But Friday after Thanksgiving was the traditional day for tree cutting. What was she supposed to do? She managed a weak smile. "That was the deal, right?"

Calvin whooped and grabbed Cyan by the hand. "Come *on*, Mr. Cyan. Let's go see the horses now. And then later, I can show you how to cut down a Christmas tree."

Cyan chuckled and winked in Maria's direction as he was tugged away. "Bye."

Maria's heart skipped a beat and she chided herself for being ridiculous. "I've got this, Betsy. I'll be over to the house in about an hour?"

"Of course. There's no rush." Betsy paused, studying Maria's face. "You know we love you like you were our own, don't you?"

Maria smiled. "Of course."

Betsy shook her head. "I can hear you thinking 'just say what it takes to get her to leave,' so I'll go. But it's the truth. Take a few minutes for yourself once you get the laundry started, I know the past couple of days haven't been easy."

That was perhaps the understatement of the year. Her eyes burned and the seemingly ever-present tears threatened yet again. Maria nodded. It was good to have people around her who loved her. "Thanks. I'll be over at the main house in an hour."

"Make it an hour and a half. I'm serious." Betsy patted Maria's shoulder before turning and hurrying toward the main house.

Maria shut the cabin door and leaned against it, closing her eyes. This was the new normal. She could do it. She had to.

7

Cyan chuckled as Calvin made kissing noises to try and attract the attention of one of the horses. The beasts were enormous. At least they seemed friendly. Cyan's experience with horses could be narrowed down to seeing them on TV. Or in movies.

The big brown one with a white stripe down its nose whickered and came to the edge of the stall.

"That's Blaze. She's sweet." Calvin reached up and patted her nose.

Tentatively, Cyan followed suit. She was softer than he'd imagined. A whuff of warm air traveled over his hand. "Hey, girl. Hi."

"Who's out—oh, hey Calvin." The man stared at Cyan for a moment before nodding. "Cyan, right?"

"Yeah. And you're Morgan?"

The man nodded. "Nice to meetcha. This little scamp showing you the ropes?"

"That was the plan. We've met Blaze."

"She's never met a stranger. I'll bring you some apple slices so no one feels left out. Give a shout if you need something. Calvin pretty much knows what to do. No going in with any of them, right champ?"

"Yes sir, Mr. Morgan."

Morgan grinned and disappeared back where he'd been working. After a moment, he reappeared with a bag that he handed to Calvin. "It's good to see you back home."

Calvin frowned. "You knew I was sick?"

"Of course. I had to figure out why my helper was missing." Morgan winked at the boy. "But you're all good now, right?"

Calvin shrugged. "I guess. Lotta needles and a pokey pen and it makes Mama cry."

Cyan's heart broke for the boy and his mom. "She'll be all right. It's hard to see someone you love hurting. Your mom? It's pretty obvious she loves you a lot."

Morgan nodded—approval? "I heard we're hooking up the sleigh later for some tree cutting. You make sure you teach Cyan here the right way to choose a tree."

"You can't come?" Calvin frowned.

"Nope. Joaquin, Tommy, and I all went out and got trees yesterday. You know we have work to do."

Calvin sighed. "Mr. Hewitt never lets me drive like you do."

Cyan hid a grin. He'd have a chat with his grandfather and see if he couldn't work something out.

Morgan ruffled the boy's hair. "You'll still have fun. Why don't you start distributing those apple slices though? Everybody's getting anxious."

It was true. More horse noses appeared in their stalls, big brown eyes turned in their direction. Morgan gave a sketch of a salute before disappearing again. Cyan glanced down at Calvin and tapped his shoulder. "So, how do we do this?"

"You've never fed a horse Mr. Cyan?"

"Never."

The boy grinned and pulled apple pieces from the bag. "It's easy. You just gotta not be scared. Watch."

Cyan stood a step behind while Calvin offered the first slice of apple to Blaze. She lipped it gently from his palm and sniffed around for more.

"Now you try."

Cyan took the slice of apple and mimicked the motion Calvin had made. It tickled ever so slightly when Blaze took the food. He grinned down at Calvin. "I see why you do this."

Calvin giggled. "Come on. You'll want to meet Socks, too."

They made their way down the row of stalls, Calvin chattering about each horse as they rubbed noses and offered apple slices. For his first experience with horses, it was pleasant. Calvin was a good guide. Did Maria realize how special her son was? Of course she did. She wasn't stupid or oblivious. From what he'd observed, she was the kind of mom who was involved in her kid's life because she wanted to be.

When the apple was gone, they dropped the bag off in what looked like an office of some sort there in the stables and headed back toward the main house. Calvin was slowing as he walked.

"You okay?"

Calvin nodded. "Getting tired."

Cyan frowned. "Want a piggyback ride the rest of the way?"

"Really? Okay!"

Cyan hunched down and caught Calvin's arms as he jumped up on his back. He hitched him up, settling his weight better, and hooked his arms around the boy's legs. "Hang on."

They reached Calvin's cabin just as Maria was stepping out the front door.

"Oh, no. Calvin. Are you okay?" Maria rushed over and reached for her son, tugging him down from Cyan's back.

"He got a little tired on the walk back. I thought a ride might be more fun."

"It was, Mama. He's good at piggyback rides." Calvin grinned up at him. "Thanks, Mr. Cyan."

"Yes, thank you." Maria turned and her deep brown eyes met and held his for one long heartbeat before she broke the contact and squatted at Calvin's level. "Let's go check your blood sugar, then, if you're okay, maybe you can help me with the potatoes for tomorrow."

Cyan tucked his hands in his pocket. "Anything I can do to help?"

Maria shook her head. "No, but I appreciate the offer."

"Okay. If you change your mind, you know where to find me. See ya, Calvin." Cyan waved and turned toward the main house. Maria seemed determined to do it all on her own. It was admirable. And infuriating. Maybe it was better—he had to leave for New York after Christmas, there was no point in getting attached. Except that he'd be back. And Calvin had already stolen his heart. His mom wasn't too far behind.

Cyan woke early and wandered out into the living room. The enormous tree they'd found and chopped—and hadn't that been more work than he'd expected?—stood in the corner. Maria had begged off from the excursion, leaving the choosing of a tree for their cabin completely in Calvin's hands. Wayne had steered him toward something appropriate for the smaller space and the boy had been delighted to show Cyan how to use the saw to get through the trunk. Both trees had one side that was fairly sparse, but as Betsy pointed out, they went in a corner so it didn't matter.

When they'd returned home, Maria had bustled Calvin off to bed. Betsy said she was too tired to decorate, so the tree had been set in its stand and left. Presumably they'd spend a good bit of time this afternoon stringing lights and hanging decorations. The whole thing wasn't something Cyan usually bothered with.

Growing up, Christmas had been an extravaganza of gifts. His parents had pushed the idea of Santa, going so far as to insist the kids were wrong when they started to figure out the truth of where all the presents came from. Only grudgingly had they ever admitted the truth, and even then, he'd had to play along or get nothing.

Since he'd left home, he took the time to send something small to each of his siblings, but other than that? It was just a built-in day off. Now, having started reading through the Gospels, he was beginning to get a glimpse of why Azure thought it mattered. If it was true that Jesus—God made man—had come to Earth to save people, then his birth would absolutely be something worth celebrating. It was the beginning of the whole story.

He sighed and settled in one of the comfortable leather chairs, digging his cell out of his pocket and thumbing open the Bible app. A notice at the top congratulated him for connecting with God's word thirty days in a row. Thirty? Really? In many ways, he'd started reading simply so he could tell Azure he was without lying. He hated to lie. Now it seemed to have become a habit. And a god who cared about people didn't seem like such a far-fetched notion. But how did one go about believing?

A light in the kitchen came on, and Cyan turned. Maria hadn't seemed to notice him, so he took the opportunity to watch her move around, deftly prepping the coffee. She didn't look like she'd slept all that well. That wasn't to say she wasn't still the most beautiful woman he'd seen in a long, long time, but she looked tired. And a little sad. Was it any wonder with what she'd gone through this week?

She opened the fridge and pulled out an enormous turkey. After setting it on the counter she stood as if frozen for several seconds before covering her face with her hands. Her shoulders began to shake silently, and Cyan looked away. Should he go to her? Or would she be embarrassed?

It didn't matter. He stood, set his phone on the arm of the chair, padded into the kitchen, and wrapped his arms around her.

Maria stiffened and struggled to pull away.

"Shh. Hey." Cyan loosened his grip and tried to catch her eye. "It's okay to let go. Probably good for you."

Tears continued to course down her cheeks as Maria shook her head. "It doesn't help anything."

"Sure it does, it helps you let out stress before it eats you from the inside out. Add a friend's shoulder into the mix and maybe you even feel better afterward." He reached up and gently brushed the tears off her cheek.

Her eyes widened.

Cyan's heart was lost. Did she have any idea how incredible she was? "I'd be honored to be that shoulder."

Maria took a deep breath, and her eyes shuttered. She was going to refuse. Push him away again. Without thinking, Cyan lowered his mouth to hers. He'd meant it to be a brief, friendly kiss, but her lips drew him in. He pulled her closer, watching as her eyes fluttered closed and she leaned in, her arms curving around his shoulders, her fingers toying with the ends of his hair. Maybe it was a good thing he hadn't managed that haircut after all.

Heart hammering in his chest, he eased back and searched her face.

"I—I'm so sorry. I'm not sure what just happened."

Cyan smiled. "I'm pretty sure I kissed you. And you kissed me back."

She licked her lips. "Obviously. I shouldn't have—this can't—you know what? I have work I need to do. You're in my way."

Her protests sounded half-hearted at best, but Cyan stepped back. "Can I just say one thing, and then I'll get out of your hair?"

Maria started ripping open the bag that held the turkey. "Go ahead."

"I'd like to be here for you, if you'll let me. As a friend. As more. Either one, though after that kiss, I'd prefer the second option. Think about it, would you, and let me know?" Cyan touched her cheek and ran his thumb over her lips before he turned and left the kitchen. He could practically feel her gaze on him as he grabbed his cell off the chair in the living room and headed down the hall to the bedroom he was using. Everything in him screamed to turn around, but he fought it. He'd made a move, now it was up to her to make one in return.

"Come in."

Wayne pushed open the door to Cyan's room and leaned on the jamb. "You coming out? There's still coffee."

He needed coffee like he needed his next breath, but he hadn't wanted to be alone with Maria again. Well, that wasn't true. He *absolutely* wanted to be alone with Maria. She just might not feel the same. "How's Thanksgiving lunch prep going? I don't want to be in the way."

Wayne chuckled. "Turkey's in the oven from the smell of it. I don't imagine Maria'll be back over for the rest of the food until about an hour before we eat. She usually makes the pies in her kitchen so Calvin can help or, if he gets bored, watch TV."

Cyan set his laptop aside and swung his legs over the side of the bed. "In that case, I could use coffee. Maybe a bowl of cereal?"

"We can do both of those things." Wayne fell into step beside him and cleared his throat. "I, uh, happened to be up early this morning."

Cyan's whole body went hot.

Wayne chuckled. "Seems to me that you gave her something to think about. Something she's been missing in her life for a long time. I can't say I'd mind having her become part of the family, but son, she's got a strong faith. As much as I love you, I hope—and believe—she's not going to let you into her life that way until you've at least accepted Jesus as your savior."

"Maybe you'd like to take a look at this while I fix myself some coffee." Cyan swiped his phone and handed it to Wayne. After he'd left the kitchen, he'd texted Azure. It hadn't been a huge surprise to find her already up and willing to chat. In the end, he wasn't able to convince himself it was worth putting off anymore. Whatever objections—maybe concerns was a better word—he'd had about Christianity paled in comparison to the pull in his heart, so he'd asked her the question he'd asked himself that morning: how did he go about believing. He smiled as he took a mug down from the cabinet and filled it at the coffee pot.

"You did this? Prayed to ask Jesus to be your savior?" Wayne held the phone back out to Cyan, his eyes shining.

"This morning, yeah."

"Because of Maria?"

"No, sir. I can't say she wasn't an influence at all, but then so are you and Grandma." Cyan splashed peppermint mocha flavored creamer into his coffee and gave it a stir.

Wayne pulled Cyan into a back-slapping hug and kissed his cheek. "You drink that coffee, I'm going to go find Betsy and tell her the news."

Cyan carried his mug to the bar. Should he get a bowl of cereal? He frowned and took an orange from the bowl of fruit on the counter instead. There was going to be a lot of food at lunch from what he'd seen in the fridge, might as well eat light now.

"Really?" Betsy hurried across the living room her arms outstretched.

Cyan ducked his head. Was everyone going to be like this? "It's not a big deal, Grandma."

Her eyes filled. "Yes it is. Oh, honey."

Cyan glanced at Wayne, imploring him to step in. He'd already dealt with one crying woman today—and, granted, that had turned out well up to the end—but he couldn't exactly solve the problem the same way with his grandmother.

"Bets, give the boy some air, you're embarrassing him." Wayne took Betsy's hand and tugged her closer so he could slip his arm around her waist.

"You told Azure?"

Cyan nodded at his grandmother. Apparently Wayne hadn't been super forthcoming with details. Then again, maybe she hadn't given him time. If he'd led off with the fact that Cyan had accepted Jesus, Betsy probably took off before he could get another word out.

"And on Thanksgiving. Or, well, close enough. Something to be truly thankful for." Betsy beamed at him before noticing the coffee and orange in front of him. "Are you just now having breakfast?"

He nodded.

"I'll let you get back to it. Wayne and I are going to haul out the decorations for the tree. Oh, Cyan." Betsy cradled his cheek in her hand for one brief moment. "I'm so happy for you."

Cyan smiled as his grandparents left the room, arm in arm. He wanted that with someone. He reached for his coffee and sipped. Not just anyone. He wanted that with Maria. Was there any possibility she'd have him?

8

Maria forced herself to focus on the decorative edging of the apple pie. If she let her mind wander, her thoughts zoomed back to kissing Cyan in the kitchen of the main house. What had she been thinking?

Obviously, she'd been thinking that, aside from not being a believer, Cyan was exactly her type. In many ways, he reminded her of Calvin's father. If that wasn't a recipe for disaster, she didn't know what one was. She'd had chemistry with him, too. She was stronger in her faith now. Stronger as a person. Stronger, in general. An amazing kiss wasn't going to get her to turn her back on everything she stood for.

And that kiss had been amazing.

She blew out a breath and glanced into the small living room where Calvin was hanging ornaments on the branches of the tree he could reach. "How's it going, Cal?"

He turned and looked at her, grinning. "Do you like it?"

"Love it. You're doing a great job."

"Are you almost ready to come help with the top part?"

"Almost, baby. Let me get this pie in the oven."

He frowned. "I'm not a baby."

"You're *my* baby." Maria winked at her little boy and carried the apple pie to the oven. He was getting more and more bothered by her calling him baby these days. Or saying he was cute. Why did they have to grow up so fast?

In her daydreams, she'd always pictured having a whole brood of kids. With more than one, there'd probably be at least one who'd put up with being called baby, wouldn't there?

Did Cyan want a big family?

What was she thinking? It didn't matter what Cyan wanted. He could worry about that with whatever woman he married. Or shacked up with. Or whatever. It wasn't her concern, so she didn't care. She ignored the stabbing pain in her heart at the thought of Cyan with someone else and dusted her hands on her jeans.

"All right, Cal, I'll get the step ladder and you hand me up the ornaments. Deal?"

"Deal!" Calvin danced in place while she dragged their step stool out of the coat closet and set it up beside the tree. He held up a clay circle with their handprints pressed into it. "This one first, Mama."

Maria smiled and looped the twine over a branch. Calvin had been three when they made that impression and it was always the first one he handed her when they got the top branches of the tree. "What's next?"

"This one."

She took the clay nativity and hung it.

"Can we put the star up top?"

"Don't you want to get all the ornaments on first?" That was their usual pattern. It didn't matter, really, but the potential break from tradition caused a little clutch in her heart.

"Okay, if you want." Calvin frowned at the pile of ornaments at his feet and selected the next for her to hang.

It didn't take long before they were down to the star. Maria wobbled a little as she stretched to reach the very top branch to affix the crowning glory. "You got a big one this year."

Calvin grinned. "Mr. Hewitt said the same thing. But Mr. Cyan helped cut it down. He has good muscles. Do you think he'll help again next year?"

A vision of herself wrapped in Cyan's arms in front of a different Christmas tree flitted through Maria's thoughts. She pushed it away and climbed down the step ladder. "I don't know, honey. He doesn't live here. Come on, we should check your blood sugar."

He pouted. "Do we have to?"

"You know we do. Until we get a better handle on how this works, okay?" Maria loaded a test strip into the glucose monitor and prepped the spring-loaded pen that would prick his finger for the necessary blood drop. "Ready?"

Calvin took a deep breath and turned his head.

Maria fought the tears that tried to well up. She'd tested it on her own finger, so she knew it wasn't really painful, but it was still not something a child should have to deal with. She squeezed his finger and pressed the drop onto the test strip. "See? All done. Go wash your hands again."

With a sigh, Calvin slid off the kitchen stool and headed down the hallway. Maria glanced at the readout and recorded the time and blood sugar number in the little notebook they were keeping. She needed to figure out a way to afford the pump with the continuous glucose monitor. She just didn't happen to have ten thousand dollars lying around. Betsy and Wayne were contacting the insurance company to see if there wasn't something that could be done. Even if it meant switching to a different plan, the peace of mind would be worth the extra monthly cost. She'd find that in the budget somehow.

Closing the notebook, Maria pushed it aside. She was doing a lot of that today. Wasn't Thanksgiving supposed to be a time of focusing on the blessings God had given? Not that she wasn't trying to do that every day, but at this time of year, it seemed so much more important. Maybe even a little easier. After all, Thanksgiving kicked off the season of celebrating Jesus' birth, and *that* was something she would forever be grateful for.

Did Cyan understand the importance? If he did, how could he not believe?

The oven timer buzzed. Maria reached for potholders and, yet again, forced her thoughts away from Cyan. And his kiss.

"Do I really have to go back to school tomorrow?" Calvin frowned at Maria as she tucked his folder into his backpack.

"You really do." She'd love to keep him home another week to make sure they had the basics of this disease under control, but he'd have to go back eventually, and, if the doctors were to be believed, that was going to mess things up anyway. So they might as well tackle the new learning curves all at once. Right? Her stomach twisted. Was it the right thing? This was the part of single parenting she hated the most. Every decision rested entirely on her shoulders. For good or for ill, it was all going to be her fault.

"What about my shots?"

She smiled and patted the couch next to her. Calvin shuffled over and flopped down. She slipped her arm around his shoulders and tugged him against her side. "I'll drive you in tomorrow and go visit the nurse. You'll have to go see her before lunch and she'll check your blood sugar and give you your shot. Hopefully before too long, we'll get you that pump the doctor was talking about and it'll get easier. For now, we'll do the best we can. You remember what it feels like when you start to get low?"

He gave a hesitant nod.

"If that happens, tell your teacher and she'll send you to the nurse."

Calvin sighed. "I'm going to live in the nurse's office."

Maria laughed. "It might feel like that for a little while, but we'll get it figured out. Promise."

"Mr. Cyan was homeschooled. Why can't I be? Then you could just take care of me."

"Oh, sweetie. That could be fun, but you know I have work, right? You've seen how busy I am on your days off— teacher work days, that sort of thing? It's like that every day. When would I teach you? And what would you do after we finished with the teaching but before I was done with all the jobs Mr. and Mrs. Hewitt need me to do? Homeschooling works for some people, but not for everyone." How on earth had that conversation started? She'd seen Calvin and Cyan chatting before and after church, and Calvin had spent a lot of his afternoon over at the main house while Maria caught a quick nap. Obviously, Cyan had been her son's primary source of entertainment.

"If you got married, could you do it then?"

Maria frowned. "I thought you liked school."

Calvin shrugged. "It's okay. I like being here better. I could help with the horses more, like I do in the summer."

And be underfoot in the stables. The guys were understanding. Maybe they even enjoyed Calvin a little. But every day? She didn't see that going over very well. "Well. For the foreseeable future, you're going to be at school. All right?"

"I guess. Can I go over and say goodnight to Mr. Cyan?"

Mr. Cyan this. Mr. Cyan that. She could understand the fascination, but it wasn't a good idea to get too attached. "I don't think so, kiddo. Why don't you go get ready for bed and then we can read a chapter or two from *The Lion, the Witch, and the Wardrobe*?"

"Three chapters?"

She chuckled. "Let's start with one and see how we're doing, okay?"

Calvin nodded and scurried off to his room.

Maria pressed her fingers to her eyes.

At a light tap on the door, she pushed herself off the couch and crossed the room. Seeing Cyan standing there in jeans and a flannel shirt made her blink. How did he look so good in something so ordinary?

"Hi." He smiled and held out a thermos. "I'm told you do bedtime stories about this time. I thought maybe hot chocolate would go well with them."

"Oh. Well, normally. But—"

"Sugar free." His teeth chattered.

"Sorry, come in. It's freezing out there." Maria stepped back to make room. Why hadn't he put on a coat? They were supposed to get more snow tonight—possibly up to half a foot.

Cyan pulled the door closed behind him. "Was it a bad idea? I just hoped—that is, it's been a long time since I heard a bedtime story."

He wanted to stay. Maria's mouth went dry. It was fine while Calvin was awake. She was getting used to that. Almost. But with Cal in his jammies, the quiet, almost intimate time snuggling with Narnia on the couch? That was what family should feel like.

"I'll go. I'm sorry. I didn't mean to overstep." Cyan turned and reached for the doorknob then paused, looking back at her over his shoulder. "I like you, Maria. A lot. And Calvin? I fell for him almost immediately. If you want me to back off completely, you're going to have to tell me that. And it'd go down a lot easier if you'd include an explanation of why."

Her heart hammered against her ribs. She cast around for the words she needed, finally managing to whisper, "You don't believe in Jesus."

"I do, now, actually. Since yesterday. I know there's a lot still for me to learn. Wayne calls it growing—I'm not up on all the lingo, but I'll get there. I've always been a pretty fast study."

Maria blinked. That was unexpected news. Good news—at least for him. For her it was a little more mixed. His beliefs were her major objection. "I—congratulations?"

"Thanks." He smiled. How had she not noticed the little crinkles at the corners of his eyes before? He certainly smiled a lot. No one would ever accuse Cyan Hewitt of being taciturn. He nodded. "Good night, then."

"Stay." The word was out before she could stop herself. She reached out and laid her fingers on his arm. "I'll get some mugs for that cocoa. You any good at reading aloud?"

"As it happens, my sisters all used to beg me for bedtime stories. Are you sure?"

Was she? A new believer was still an iffy proposition, but at least it was a step in the right direction. It wasn't as if a bedtime story was a diamond ring. She nodded and pointed to the couch. "Have a seat. I'll check on Calvin and get the drinks."

"How's my grandson at reading?" Betsy leaned her hip against the kitchen island and waggled her eyebrows.

Maria set aside the cloth she was using to wipe the counters and sighed. "Better than me. He does voices for the characters. Good ones. I don't think Calvin will ever be satisfied with me reading again."

Betsy chuckled. "I doubt that. He loves you."

"He loves Cyan, too."

"Does he? How do you know?"

Maria shook her head. "He said so last night while he was praying. What am I supposed to do, Betsy?"

"What do you want to do?"

Maria frowned.

Betsy held up a hand. "I'm not being glib, I'm asking. I think what you want should be a factor. Just like what he wants should be."

What *did* she want? Maria sighed. She'd never been able to chase away dreams of marriage and a family, no matter how hard she tried. But a single mom didn't have a ton of time to date and, even if she had the time, she'd never been able to figure out how to explain it to Calvin. She was the only constant in her boy's life. Well, Wayne and Betsy were at this point, too. Throw in the unstated expectation of sex, even from the handful of Christian men she'd tried to date, and she wasn't interested. But Cyan had her rethinking things she'd thought were firmly closed. "Where is he?"

"Cyan?"

Maria nodded. Who else could she mean?

"He and Wayne went out to look at the empty cabins. Seems our grandson has it in his head to make himself a permanent base here." Betsy shot Maria a knowing look. "Can't imagine why."

He was staying here? She reached for the cloth and started scrubbing.

"Don't you like him at all?"

"Too much, Betsy. I've known him almost two weeks. I shouldn't feel this way about him. Or his kisses."

"Kisses?" Betsy made a humming noise in her throat. "He works fast."

"Don't sound so proud." Heat crept across Maria's cheeks. Why had she mentioned the kisses? Maybe because she needed to talk to someone about them and Betsy was the closest thing she had to a girlfriend. "I have no business kissing anyone, let alone Cyan."

"What's wrong with kissing Cyan?"

Maria threw her hands in the air, the cloth fluttering like a flag of surrender. "Two weeks, Betsy. And he's been a Christian for three days? How is a new believer any different than a non-believer in terms of dating? For that matter, how do I know he didn't decide to believe just because he knew it was something that mattered to me?"

"Now hold up." Betsy frowned and crossed her arms. "That boy has been edging closer to Jesus for the last year. Wayne and I—and his older sister Azure—have been praying for him constantly. I won't say knowing you cared about it wasn't another little nudge, but his decision to trust Jesus isn't about you. It's about him and Jesus."

Maria closed her eyes. Was it possible to feel any smaller? Of course it wasn't about her. "The fact that I can make all of this about me is another reason I shouldn't be thinking about Cyan that way."

"Oh, please." Betsy blew a raspberry.

Maria chuckled in spite of herself. "I'm serious."

"So am I. Cyan's a good man. He was a good man before he came to Christ, he's going to be an even better one now that he's actively seeking that relationship. You could do a whole lot worse. I'm not saying marry him tomorrow, but I am suggesting that maybe it's time you gave yourself a chance to be a young woman and not just a mom."

Maria swallowed. Did she even know how to do that anymore? Calvin, her job, and school were her life. Could she make room for Cyan? Should she? She glanced over at her friend and offered a small smile. "Any chance you and Wayne could babysit on Friday night?"

A grin split Betsy's face. "Thatta girl. I'm pretty sure we're free."

Okay. Maria drew in a deep breath. She'd half-hoped there'd be a conflict. Now she just had to figure out where she was going to work up the nerve to ask Cyan out.

9

Cyan checked the time at the bottom of his laptop's monitor and hit save. He stretched his arms up over his head and glanced around the main room of the cabin. He'd convinced Wayne to let him rent the place and they'd worked out an agreement that included a final price that was way lower than seemed reasonable. His grandfather had insisted when Cyan had made it clear he wouldn't live there for free.

At some point, he was going to have to tell his parents he'd decided to settle here. He'd considered simply saying New Mexico, generically, but that was akin to a lie, wasn't it? The easy lie had never been something he'd enjoyed. It was better by far to deal with the fallout right away, rather than compounding it.

"Sooner's better than later." Cyan blew out a breath and reached for his cell. He dialed his parents before he had time to talk himself out of it.

"Cyan! How are you, honey?" His mother sounded slightly out of breath, but happy.

"I'm good. Figured I should call and say hello."

"That's always nice. Let me get your father."

Cyan winced as his mother hollered for his dad. He'd half hoped he could let her pass on the information. Apparently he was an enormous, yellow chicken.

"Hey there Cyan, to what do we owe the pleasure?" His dad's voice held a hint of teasing, but the barb still hit home.

"Oh, honey, give it a rest. If you want to talk to him more, you know how to dial the phone. We're glad you called, Cy."

"Thanks, Mom. Hi, Dad."

"So, where are you these days? Still up in the Pacific Northwest?" His dad sighed. "It's so pretty up there, I can see why you like it."

Cyan took a deep breath. Like a bandage. Just do it fast and brace for impact. "I'm actually in New Mexico. At Rancho de Esperanza."

"That's a lovely name. Hope Ranch, isn't it?" Clearly his mother hadn't pieced it together yet. "That's a lot like...oh. Well, that's nice, right dear?"

"Nice isn't the word I'd choose." His father's voice could make ice shiver. "What are you doing there?"

"Getting to know my grandparents. It's a beautiful place. I imagine growing up here was amazing." He needed to stop babbling. He cleared his throat. "I'm actually planning on settling here."

"With my parents."

"Dad." Cyan discarded every thought as it popped into his head. "Yes. With my grandparents. I'm sorry it hurts you. They would be, too."

"Whatever. Just watch your back, they'll be dragging you to church and preaching at you constantly before you know it." His mother murmured in the background, but Cyan couldn't catch the words over his father's breathing.

Might as well get it all over with. "I don't actually mind that. I'm a Christian now, too. Like Azure."

"Oh for—here. You talk to him. What did we do wrong? That's what I want to know." There was a pause and then the bullet-like slam of a door before his mother came on the line.

"Oh, Cyan."

"I know, Mom. I'm sorry it hurts the two of you, but you raised us to be independent thinkers."

Her chuckle was resigned. "Maybe I'll try that on Dad and see if making it his fault helps any."

"I didn't mean it that way. I love you. Both of you."

"We love you too, Cy. Maybe it's better if you just text me now and then for a little while. He got over Azure's conversion, I'm sure it's just a matter of time before he's okay with yours."

Cyan pressed his fingers to his eyes. It wasn't any worse than what he'd expected. That didn't make it good. "Okay. Thanks."

"Bye, honey."

He ended the call and stared at his computer. He'd done enough work for right now. He'd wander down to the main house and scrounge up a snack. Maybe he could accidentally bump into Maria. He'd been trying to give her some space ever since he'd barged in on their story time on Sunday night. It had been harder than he'd imagined.

She hadn't sought him out, either.

They both had work. And there was Calvin. He shook his head. If he'd hoped avoiding Maria would send her chasing after him, he'd misjudged badly. Maybe it was time to try a different tactic.

Grabbing his coat, Cyan stomped into his boots and headed through the crisp, clear afternoon toward the main house. The snow had all been cleared, leaving neat paths for moving between buildings. He'd meant to offer to help, but work was picking up with one client and he hadn't gotten to it. Clearly, the guys knew what they were doing. He would likely have just been in the way. Still, he'd make a point of asking what he could do to help out around here. If it was going to be his home, he should contribute.

Cyan wiped his boots on the mat outside the kitchen door before stepping through into the mudroom. He stepped out of his shoes, leaving them with the other outside gear piled neatly by the door. Were Maria's in there? He frowned, unsure. What was he going to do if she wasn't here? He hung his coat on an empty hook and wandered out of the little mud room into the kitchen proper. It was sparkling clean. And empty.

Cyan blew out a breath. "Hello?"

No one answered. It was entirely possible they hadn't heard him. The house was large and his grandparents liked to play music while they worked in the office. Maria had headphones she slipped on while she cleaned. What did she listen to? Just one more thing he wondered. He wanted to find out everything about her.

He poked his head in the dining room—a space that was seldom used from what he'd observed. They'd eaten their delayed Thanksgiving dinner in there, but that was it. Still, everything gleamed with an air of having just been cleaned. With a frown, he turned and nearly crashed into Maria.

"Sorry." Cyan reached out a hand. "Hi."

Maria slipped her headphones off and smiled. "Hi. Are you looking for your grandparents? They went in to town. I think they're going to pick Calvin up after school and take him out to dinner."

"Oh? That's nice. I didn't realize they did that."

She shrugged. "Not a lot."

"Does that mean you're free this evening? Or were they doing that because you had plans?" It'd be just his luck that she had plans. Maybe even a date. She was beautiful, inside and out. There was probably a line of men six miles long who wanted to date her.

"I was hoping to have plans, actually. I just haven't had time to firm them up yet."

Cyan fought to keep a friendly smile on his face. Of course. Just like he thought. At least he had plenty of work to keep himself occupied. "Have fun. I'll get out of your hair and get back to work."

"No!" Maria broke off, her cheeks turning red. She cleared her throat. "You misunderstood. Or I wasn't clear. Or something. Doesn't matter. I'd asked your grandparents to watch Calvin tonight—on Monday, actually—because I was hoping you might want to go out. With me. Alone. I mean together. But without Calvin."

"You want to go out to eat?"

She nodded, her expression morphing into one of misery. "It's okay. I should've asked sooner. I kept thinking I'd bump into you, but this week has been busy, I guess. And maybe you don't even want to—it's presumptuous. I'm sorry. Just forget it. Please?"

"Wait." Cyan grabbed her hand before she could turn and, if her body language was any indication, run far, far away. He smiled. "It happens that I like eating dinner. I think I'd like eating with a beautiful woman even more. If the offer's still good?"

"You don't have to—"

Cyan pressed his lips to hers in a brief kiss that still made his pulse race. "I know that. I came over here to find you and ask you out. You beat me to the punch."

"You were going to ask me out? What about Calvin?"

His face heated. "I hadn't gotten that far yet. I'd hoped I could talk my grandparents into watching him, but if not, we'd just drag him along. He'd keep the conversation rolling, if nothing else."

"You would've taken him with? On our date?"

Cyan shrugged. "Sure, why not? He's a great kid. It might mean I didn't get to hold your hand, and that would be a bummer, but I'd probably live. Turns out though, that's not an issue."

Maria flashed a grin. "True."

"So? Dinner?"

"I'd like that. Since I technically asked you out, do I get to choose the place?"

Cyan chuckled. "Sure. I probably would've let you do that anyway since the only restaurant I know of is the fast food joint I hit on the highway on the way into town. That's not quite what I had in mind."

"Perfect." Maria pulled her phone out of her pocket and glanced at the display. "I have maybe another hour I need to get in here. Does six work for you?"

"Sure. I'll meet you at your place?"

She nodded.

He leaned forward and brushed his lips across hers, his gaze holding hers steadily. "See you then."

"What kind of food do you call that?" Cyan held the door for Maria as they exited the restaurant. "It's not really Mexican. Or, at least, not the kind of Mexican I'm used to."

Maria chuckled as she zipped her coat and tugged a knit cap down over her ears. "It's New Mexican."

"Okay. What's that?" Cyan zipped his own coat as a gust of wind reminded him that it was the start of December and they were at a higher elevation than he was used to.

"Blend of Spanish, Mexican, and Native American flavors. It's unique to the state, so it's not super surprising you've never had it before. But it's hands down my favorite."

He nodded. He'd never thought to differentiate between Spanish and Mexican, but there were obviously differences. "It was good. There's more on that menu I'd like to try."

"Then we'll come back again."

He warmed through and reached for her hand. "Want to take a walk around the square?"

Maria hesitated.

"Or we can head back." Maybe he'd misread the evening somehow, but it had seemed like she had a good time. Hadn't she just suggested they return to the restaurant? Wasn't that a second date?

"It's not that. I just—bedtime. I hate to miss Calvin's bedtime. And that's stupid. It's not as if I've never missed putting him to bed before."

"But you don't like to." Cyan dug his phone out of his pocket and checked the time. "What if we called and asked Betsy and Wayne to let him stay up an extra thirty minutes? Then we'd have enough time for a little stroll, maybe some ice cream, and you'd still get bedtime."

"Ice cream?" Maria shook her head. "You've lost your mind. It's freezing."

He shrugged. "Just means it won't melt and you can eat it slower. We can skip that, if you want."

"You can get ice cream. I'll get coffee." She edged closer so their bodies brushed. "You don't think they'll mind?"

Maria knew his grandparents better than he did, but he *did* know they adored Calvin. "Let's call and find out."

Cyan tapped his grandmother's picture in his contacts and waited as it rang. When she answered, he ran their idea by her and smiled as she quickly agreed. He offered the phone to Maria. "Want to say hi to her or Calvin first?"

Maria took the phone. "You're sure it's not a problem? He's acting okay?"

Cyan couldn't hear his grandmother fully, but from the fact that Maria's face relaxed slightly, Betsy must've been reassuring her.

"Okay. Thank you." Maria handed the phone back to Cyan.

He held it to his ear, but Betsy must have hung up. "So, a walk and a treat and then home?"

Maria offered a small smile. "Sounds good."

He would've preferred more enthusiasm, but he imagined it was tricky to balance mom life with everything else. Especially with the diabetes diagnosis thrown into the works. They walked in relative silence the block or so that took them the main square.

"What are those?" Cyan pointed to the square that was lit somehow. The white twinkle lights he'd expected were wound around tree branches, but the paths and walls were lined with something he'd never seen before.

"*Luminarias.*" Maria grinned. "We'll probably get ours up at the ranch tomorrow. We're a little behind with the outdoor decorations this year. They're paper bags with sand and candles."

"Candles in paper bags seems like a really bad idea." There was a break in the traffic, so Cyan tugged Maria across the street. "Don't they have a lot of fires?"

"No." She shrugged. "They've done this my whole life and I never thought to wonder about that. I just like the warm glow. There's nothing like it."

That, he could agree with. He squatted at the edge of the path and peered into one of the bags. A votive candle flickered merrily in a bed of sand. The bag protected the flame from the wind, so maybe there wasn't any way for the thing to catch fire. Unless it got blown over. But surely there was enough weight in the sand to keep that from happening. "Not something people leave unattended, I imagine?"

"I—maybe not? We light ours and leave them until bedtime, then put them out."

That was a lot more work than a strand of lights that could be put on a timer. "Every night?"

"Sure. Some things are worth the extra effort." Maria turned and her gaze locked with his.

His lips curved and he lost himself for a moment in her eyes. "I couldn't agree more."

10

Maria waved to Calvin as he got on the bus and waited until the door closed and the big yellow vehicle lumbered down the road. She sighed and turned, heading back down the long driveway. There was a lot to do today. There was always a lot to do, but with the weekends filling up with sleigh rides and bonfires as the community made its way up to partake of the usual Christmas cheer available at Rancho de Esperanza, it seemed like there was more.

Ranch of Hope. The name had been one of the big draws for her when Maria had been trying to figure out what to do with a life that had just careened off course. Everyone needed a little hope. She'd been here coming up on eight years now, and she saw the hope the Hewitts went out of their way to offer to everyone who crossed their path. Maybe she hadn't been a particularly strong Christian when she landed on their doorstep pregnant, but they'd helped her change that. And now they were doing the same thing for Cyan.

Her heart gave a funny little skip as her mind built a picture of him from Saturday, all tall and lanky in faded jeans and a fraying sweatshirt as he manned the s'mores station by the bonfire. He'd navigated the trouble with Calvin better than she had, too. Maria's plan was to simply cut sugar from Calvin's life. It seemed like the most certain way to avoid highs and lows—both of which could end them back in the hospital if they weren't careful. Wasn't it enough that she had to trust him to the school nurse during the day, five days a week? And that she hardly slept, she was so intent on keeping an ear open for him heading to the bathroom—a pretty sure sign his sugars were high? Of course, it wasn't as if Calvin completely got it. He was used to gorging himself on s'mores for the month of December. Since that was out, Cyan had dubbed him his official helper and put him in charge of doling out chocolate bars and marshmallows. Calvin loved it. And the couple of times he snitched a piece of chocolate, Cyan had noted it and let her know, so they'd been able to adjust, mostly, and avoid problems.

Maria slipped out of her boots in the mudroom of the big house and tugged on her sneakers. It was past time to stop thinking about Cyan and move on with her work. Today was meal planning day—and wasn't that just a thrill—so she could get to the grocery store in the afternoon and grab Calvin from school on the way home.

"There you are." Betsy sat at the counter with a huge mug of coffee and her Bible. She closed the book and pushed it aside. "Calvin off to school?"

"He is. I feel like I'm running a little behind though, so—"

"Pfft. Get yourself some coffee and sit a minute."

Maria fought a sigh and moved to the machine on the counter. Hopefully, whatever was buzzing around in Betsy's bonnet would be quick. She stirred a little sugar into her mug, decided against cream, and carried it over to the island. "What's up?"

"You have fun on Friday?"

Maria's cheeks warmed. "Sure. You know I love eating out."

"That's not quite what I meant." Betsy shook her head. "I guess you figure I'm prying."

"No. It's not that." Not exactly. Well, maybe sort of. "It's just weird talking about it."

"You told me all about the dates you went on with Tommy and Morgan when they asked you out. What's making this one weird?"

She'd known going into those dates that there wasn't any potential. Not really. She'd only gone because they were persistent and she'd wanted to maintain a good working relationship with them. But Cyan? Everything about him screamed potential, and had since she first pulled open the door to find him standing there. How, exactly, was she supposed to explain that to Betsy? "They weren't your grandson."

"I see." Betsy took a casual sip of her coffee. "You don't like the idea of being part of the family officially?"

Maria frowned. "Did I say that? Besides, one date does not a marriage make."

"True. Of course, if you don't go on dates, you don't end up with that marriage either. Unless you're going for an arranged marriage where you meet, get married, and then get to know the person?"

"Has anyone told you you're impossible lately?" Maria looked into her coffee, frowning. "I like him. A lot. Too much, maybe. I don't know what to do with that. Calvin's the result of the last impetuous dating decision I made. I can't go there again. And he makes me want to."

Betsy reached over and covered Maria's hand. "He's a good man. I understand wanting—even needing—to take it slow, but don't get so caught up in not repeating a mistake of the past that you miss out on the future God has for you. Now, tell me how Calvin's doing. Really. Because you act like you've got this diabetes thing licked and that doesn't seem completely possible."

Maria hunched her shoulders under Betsy's steady gaze. "We're muddling through. It's hard. Little boys like sweets, and I'm used to letting him have them."

"You never over did."

"No, but they weren't special treats and now they have to be. It tears me up inside every time I have to prick his finger or give him a shot—I feel like I'm a bad mother because I'm glad the school nurse has to do it during the day instead of me. And I'm so tired of dealing with the insurance company. Every single one of Calvin's doctors says he needs to be on a pump—that it'll make both of our lives easier—but the insurance company doesn't care." Maria blew out a breath. "So, how's Calvin doing? He's okay. He's resilient. His mom is struggling."

"How can I help?"

Right there was why Maria hadn't unburdened herself before. She loved that Betsy would ask—had known she was going to—but there was nothing anyone could do. She shook her head. "This is just the new normal. It takes some getting used to. We'll get there."

After a moment, Betsy nodded. "All right, then. If you think of something, let me know. I'll let you get back to your work. I know I've held you up. Do me a favor though?"

"What?"

"Take a little snack out to Cyan sometime today? He said he didn't want to intrude on lunch, because he's not an employee."

"I always make plenty." Maria frowned. What was he thinking? She'd been pinning her hopes of seeing him on that meal. Even though they weren't alone, she'd get to chat with him, maybe flirt a little. She hadn't decided on that last bit yet. Her flirting skills were pretty rusty. Throw in an audience and maybe it wasn't the best idea.

"I tried to tell him that." Betsy shrugged. "You'll take him something?"

Maria nodded. She absolutely would. It might just come with a piece of her mind on the side.

Maria knocked on the cabin door and tried the handle. When it turned, she pushed the door open and leaned in. "Cyan?"

"Come on in, I'm in the dining room."

Maria stepped in and pushed the door closed behind her. She looked around. He hadn't done anything to customize his space yet. Did he plan to? He'd said he was going to stay here permanently. He hadn't really had time to do anything about the basic sofa and hotel-quality art, but there was no clutter even. They had enough spare Christmas decorations lying around. She'd have to bring something over. He needed some seasonal cheer in here.

This cabin's layout was different from hers. The door still opened into the main living area, but arched doorways led to the kitchen straight ahead, the dining room to the left, and a hallway to bedrooms on the right. It was interesting. She'd grown used to everything being open at her place, but the separation wasn't a bad thing.

She hovered in the archway to the dining room and smiled. Cyan leaned back in one of the spindly chairs, his laptop and several stacks of paper spread out on the table in front of him. His feet were bare below the frayed hems of his jeans, and the sleeves of his light gray sweatshirt were pushed up to his elbows. Her mouth watered.

"Hi."

He grinned. "Hi, back. What brings you here?"

"Lunch. Did you eat?"

Cyan shook his head. "I was going to slap together a PB and J and call it a day."

"Poet."

"I have untapped depths." Cyan chuckled and sniffed. "Whatever you brought smells better than peanut butter."

"I should hope so." Maria hefted the insulated bag onto the table then frowned. "Is there a place to eat in the kitchen? I don't want to get your work messy."

"Sure. There are stools at the counter, but I can clear some of this away. It's nicer in here."

"I don't want to mess anything up. Give me a couple minutes to set up in there and then come eat." She backed out of the dining room and angled toward the kitchen. Stepping through the doorway she stopped, eyes widening. The kitchen was done in hues of gold and green, like some kind of nightmare from the seventies. The only thing it had going for it was that it was a small space, so at least the horror was contained. No wonder he'd wanted to eat in the dining room.

Maria glanced over her shoulder. Maybe...no. Cyan had covered the majority of the table with his stuff. Cleaning it up wouldn't be a small undertaking. Not if he needed to keep an order to the papers and piles. Why on earth hadn't the Hewitts done something about this kitchen before now?

At least it was clean.

She set the insulated bag on the counter and pulled out the containers and dishes. She hadn't known if Cyan would have plates, so she'd brought them, too. It didn't take long to set out two portions of the tamales, rice, and beans that she'd made for lunch. She was just adding a sprinkle of cheese to the beans when Cyan padded in.

"Are those tamales?" He sniffed and his eyes closed. "Yum. Where'd you get them?"

"Get them?" Maria fought the urge to bristle. "I made them. People do, you know."

"Not anyone I've ever met." He grinned and hopped onto one of the stools. "Just one more way you're amazing. This definitely tops peanut butter."

She couldn't help but chuckle. "Just about anything would."

"No. No no no. You're not a peanut butter snob, are you? That's a pretty major flaw." Cyan shook his head. "The things you find out about people."

"Seriously? It's mashed up peanuts. What's appetizing about that?" She took her own seat and reached for the napkin she'd set beside her plate. "Before you answer, you want to pray?"

He gave her a startled glance. "Oh. Um. Sure? Unless you want to?"

"You go ahead." Fighting a smile, she folded her hands in her lap and closed her eyes. When several seconds passed in silence, she opened one lid and glanced at him. "You know how, right? It doesn't have to be fancy."

Pink tinged his cheeks and he hunched his shoulders. "I've never done it out loud. The whole praying thing is new to me, you realize?"

She nodded. "Good practice for you then. I'm a safe audience, I promise. No judgment."

His Adam's apple bobbed as he swallowed before bowing his head. "Um. Thank you, Jesus, for this food. And um, bless the hands that prepared it. They belong to a pretty special woman. Amen."

Her cheeks were warm. He thought she was special. That shouldn't be a surprise. Cyan was pretty free with his compliments. Somehow, they always seemed sincere, too. "Why aren't you coming to lunch at the main house?"

He shrugged. "I don't want to be in the way. Plus, I don't usually take a very long lunch break. I'd rather plow through my hours and then be done. Why?"

"Maybe I was looking forward to seeing you."

"Yeah?"

She nodded and peeled back the tamale wrapper with her fork. Should she not have said that? Was it too bold?

"That was the downside, certainly." He reached over and covered her hand with his. "I thought you might want some space. I got that vibe on Saturday night. With the s'mores?"

"Really? That was absolutely not my intention."

"Okay." He forked up a big bite. "I thought maybe I'd overstepped by giving Calvin a job. He's just really bummed about the sugar restrictions."

"I know." Maria sighed. "We've got to find our way. It's not realistic to think he can never eat anything sweet again. I mean, when he goes low, he has to, but I don't want him to think he has to be having a blood sugar crisis in order to get a treat. It's a mess, and I feel like I'm bungling it constantly."

Cyan squeezed her hand before letting go. "You're not. Not from where I'm sitting at least. Like you said, you're still figuring it out. And I think you're doing great."

Maria smiled. "That's because you like me."

"Probably factors in, doesn't change the truth of it. Speaking of that, though."

Her stomach tightened. That wasn't usually a good opener. "What?"

"I was thinking I should go do a little Christmas shopping. I don't want to do everything online. It's not as personal. Plus, my siblings give me grief when their gifts arrive in a store box. I thought maybe you and Calvin might want to join me? Betsy was saying how my best bet was going to be Santa Fe, or maybe even Albuquerque."

"The mall?"

He nodded.

Maria hadn't finished all of her shopping yet. Calvin's new diagnosis had thrown off her schedule. She'd planned to just get online and knock it out, but she loved seeing the mall all decorated. Calvin still enjoyed getting a photo with Santa. She didn't really do the whole Santa thing with him, never had, but even though Calvin knew Christmas was about Jesus, they both enjoyed the photo with a man in a red suit. "When?"

"What works for you? I'm pretty flexible."

Saturdays were getting busier now that they were firmly into December. "Maybe Sunday after church if we can hit the early service? It's a long drive, but since there's nothing happening at the ranch that evening we wouldn't be in a rush to get back."

"Sure. That works." He scraped the last of the food off his plate. "This was really good. Thanks for bringing it over."

"I'm glad you liked it." She hesitated. Was it too forward to ask about Friday? No. They were past that. Weren't they? "Are you helping with the bonfire again this weekend?"

He nodded. "That's the plan. Can I use Calvin again?"

"He'd probably love that. Would you like to join us for supper beforehand?"

"Absolutely. Could I maybe come tonight for more bedtime reading? I haven't actually read the Narnia books before. I liked it."

"You really never read them? Saw the movies? Not that the movies are all that great, mind you, but still. It's not like they're obscure."

"Nope."

"Sure. We'd love to have you. No cocoa this time, though. Even if it is sugar free."

He laughed. "Yes ma'am."

Maria slid off the stool. "I can let you get back to work. I'll tidy up here and let myself out. You're going to do something about this kitchen, right?"

"As soon as I take up full time residence, it's going to be first."

"Why aren't you living here?"

"Wayne asked me to stay through Christmas at the big house. It gives us a chance to know each other better. Since it looks like I'm going to have to head out on travel right after the holidays, it's just as easy to wait and get settled when I'm back than start and interrupt the progress."

She frowned. "You're leaving?"

"For work, yeah. I was trying to get out of it, but that doesn't look like it's worked. So, yeah. Probably just after the new year."

"When will you be back?" The way he talked about it, Maria didn't think it was going to be a short trip.

"Best case scenario? Mid-March."

"And worst case?" She wrapped her arms around herself. Why hadn't he said something about this sooner? Here she was bringing him into her life—into Calvin's life—building all sorts of fantasies about the future, and he was planning to leave.

"Probably mid-May."

May. Five months. She gave a stiff nod. "I see."

"I didn't want to say anything until I knew for sure." Cyan frowned. "It's not like I want to go. Don't be mad. Please?"

She shook her head. It was a good reminder that for all of the confused and mixed up feelings she had for Cyan, she didn't know him. Not really. Better to take things slow. There was too much at stake to rush headlong into love. "I'm not mad. Just surprised, I guess. Get back to work. I should be getting back myself."

He studied her before nodding. "It's still okay if I come for the bedtime story?"

Maria nodded. "Of course."

Calvin would be elated. So, despite everything, would she.

11

Cyan frowned at the mugs in his hands. Should he take them back? Maria had said no hot chocolate. This wasn't hot chocolate. And it was still sugar free. Besides, it was Christmas. Or almost. If a kid couldn't have a few extra treats at Christmastime, what was the point?

Sure, okay. Jesus. He got that now. But still. With a grunt, he knocked on Maria's cabin door. If she said no, he'd take the lumps. Everything in him wanted to spoil Calvin a little. The kid was a champ. From what he'd seen, Calvin was handling this new diagnosis better than his mom was. Of course, at seven, Calvin didn't have to deal with the details.

Maria's smile was strained as she opened the door. Her gaze flicked to the mugs and she shook her head. "Come on in. We're fighting a low. Maybe that'll help."

"A low?" Cyan entered and kicked the door closed behind him.

"Blood sugar. I don't know if I calculated dinner wrong or he just didn't eat everything or what. His plate was empty, but he's sneaky. And he doesn't like the rice when I make it with chiles in it. But I said—"

"I don't care what you said." Calvin crossed his arms, scowling at his mother from the couch.

Maria sighed. "I said he had to eat it. I thought he had. Drink your juice, Cal."

"Don't want juice. I want candy."

"Too bad. Drink the juice." Maria pinned him with her gaze before turning to Cyan. "I don't know if we're even going to get to bedtime stories tonight. Is that hot chocolate?"

Cyan shook his head. "Eggnog. But it's sugar free, too."

"Just put it in the kitchen, would you? We can reheat it if someone ever cooperates enough to get to a healthy range." Maria frowned at her son.

Cyan did as instructed then stood, unsure. Was there a way to help? Or was he just in the way? "Do you want me to go?"

"Maybe it'd be—"

"No!" Calvin jumped off the couch and flung himself at Cyan.

Cyan pried Calvin's arms away and squatted so they were eye level. "Tell you what. You drink that juice and I'll stay. Maybe if you do a good job, your mom'll still let you have a bedtime story."

Calvin pouted but stuck the straw of the juice box in his mouth and sucked. "I don't like fruit punch."

Maria threw her hands in the air. "What am I supposed to do? The bigger packages come as a variety pack. It's cheaper that way. We have to drink all the kinds before I can buy more. This is always last. It's all I have right now."

Cyan hefted Calvin up onto his hip as the boy drained the juice box and crossed to Maria. The tears brimming in her eyes broke his heart. He wanted—well, he wanted to kiss her and tell her everything would be all right. But he couldn't promise that. There wasn't really even anything he could do—at least not that he could think of—to help.

Calvin slurped the last bits of juice out of the box and stuck out his tongue.

Cyan set him on the couch and took the empty box. "Good job, bud."

Maria squeezed the bridge of her nose. "I can take that."

"I got it. Why don't you sit?"

She shook her head and wrapped her arms around her waist. "Can't."

Cyan pressed his lips together and carried the juice box to the kitchen. He tossed it in the recycle bin and crossed to Maria. He rubbed his hands up her arms. "Now what?"

"Now we wait. Ten minutes or so and we test his sugar again and see where it is. Why didn't he just eat the rice?" Her voice was low and she kept looking over at Calvin on the couch.

"He's seven." Cyan hadn't eaten anything he didn't like when he was seven. His mom and dad tried everything to get him to try new things. Never worked. Honestly, he wasn't super excited about doing it as an adult and only really did when he had to be polite.

"I know, it's just—" She shook her head again. "How am I supposed to keep him healthy?"

"Exactly the way you are. You'll compromise when you need to and adjust when you must." Cyan jerked his head toward the couch. "Come on, let's sit. We'll start reading and you can do the blood sugar thing when it's time. Want some eggnog?"

She wrinkled her nose. "Not really ever."

"Seriously? It's like the official drink of Christmas. How can you not want it?"

Maria made a face. "Nope."

"Your loss. Mind if I have mine?"

"Nah. I'll get the book."

"Are you gonna read, Mr. Cyan?" Calvin popped his head over the top of the sofa.

He was perkier. That had to be good, didn't it? Maybe the juice was doing its trick. "Sure am, champ. Just as soon as your mom gets the book."

"Here we go." Maria handed the book to Cyan and settled on the couch next to Calvin. "How do you feel, baby?"

Calvin shrugged. "Will you do the voices again? They're at the beavers' house and mom doesn't separate Mr. and Mrs. Beaver very well."

Cyan shot Maria an apologetic look.

Maria rolled her eyes.

"I'll see what I can do. Ready?"

Calvin nodded.

Cyan flipped open the book at the right spot and began to read. He wasn't completely sure what had happened since the last time he was here for bedtime reading. Obviously, all the Pevensie children had now made it into Narnia, but how? He was going to have to order a copy for himself. That'd give him a leg up on deciding what sorts of other voices he might need, too.

While he read, Maria took Calvin's hand and used something that looked like a pen to prick his finger, catching the little drop of blood with a skinny piece of plastic that stuck out of a pager-sized device. When it beeped, she frowned a moment and rose, returning to the couch with another juice box.

"Aw, Mom."

"Shh. Drink it. You're still too low."

Shoulders slumping, Calvin jabbed the straw into the little hole.

Cyan patted the boy's leg as he read. When he reached the end of the chapter, he stuck his finger in the pages and glanced at Maria. "More? Or do we have to stop."

"One more, please Mom? I need to know where Edmund went. He's a jerk."

"Calvin. We don't call people that." Maria frowned.

"But he is." Calvin's lower lip poked out.

Cyan smothered a laugh. The kid was right. So far, there was nothing really to recommend Edmund. Maybe he got turned into a statue. That seemed to be a distinct possibility, and it'd serve the brat right. "So? Can we find out where he went? Although I have a pretty good idea, don't you Cal?"

"He probably snuck off to see the stupid witch and eat more Turkish Delight. Mom looked it up on the Internet and showed me a picture. It sounds gross. Why would anyone want to eat it?"

Cyan chuckled. He'd been curious enough to look it up, too, after the last reading session. It didn't look like a treat he'd particularly enjoy. "All I can say is people in other countries like different things. You know, I'll bet if we could offer Edmund one of our famous s'mores, he might not like them."

"No way. We make the best s'mores." Calvin grinned up at Cyan, and Cyan's heart turned to mush.

"We sure do. Even my grandpa commented on how much better they are this year now that you're helping."

"Yeah? Mr. Hewitt said that?" The boy's eyes lit and he turned to Maria. "I told you I was helping."

"Of course you are." Cyan glanced at Maria. "Why would anyone think otherwise?"

"I just didn't want him to be in the way." Maria seemed to shrink into herself. "Or bother anyone."

Bother anyone. Bother Cyan was obviously what she meant. Cyan frowned. "I suspect everyone out there is honest enough to say if Cal's in the way. Which he isn't."

"Okay." Maria sighed. "Why doesn't Cyan read one more chapter, and then we'll check your sugar again? Deal?"

Calvin grinned and nodded. He snuggled up against Cyan's side.

Cyan slid his arm around the boy and opened the book. "Maybe Edmund'll get eaten by a wolf."

Calvin giggled.

Maria opened her mouth then snapped it shut, shaking her head.

When the chapter was finished and Maria had confirmed Calvin's blood sugar was where it needed to be before bed, Cyan tucked the bookmark between the pages and stood. "Thanks for letting me read with you. I'm going to have to get my own copy so I don't miss anything."

"Go brush your teeth, baby, I'll be there in a minute." Maria patted her son's leg.

Calvin hopped off the couch and flung his arms around Cyan. "I'm glad you could come read tonight. If I didn't have to go to school, I could hang out with you all day."

"Yeah? You know what I do all day?"

Calvin shook his head.

"I work on my computer. It's not very interesting."

Calvin frowned. "Oh."

"I don't even like to listen to music. I need to concentrate. I bet school's a little more interesting."

"We get art tomorrow."

"See? That's way more fun."

"Okay. But I can still help with s'mores on Friday?"

"If your Mom says it's okay, it's okay with me. Why don't we see what the end of the week brings, okay?" Cyan ruffled Calvin's hair. "Go brush your teeth like your mom told you. I'll see you again later."

Calvin waved and darted down the hall.

"Sorry—"

Cyan cut Maria off. "I enjoy him. And you."

Pink stained Maria's cheeks. "I don't know what to do when you say things like that."

Cyan handed her the book and stepped close. He brushed his lips across hers. "See you tomorrow."

"You ready, buddy?" Cyan hunched so half his face was hidden in the collar of his heavy winter jacket and glanced over at Calvin. They hadn't had any more snow this week, but it was still cold. Once the sun went down, it got even colder. Still, the residents of the area—and maybe some of the folks in town to ski on the semi-famous slopes nearby—flocked to the ranch to partake of some Christmas cheer. Morgan and Tommy were running the sleigh rides. One went out to the area Cyan's grandparents had marked off for folks who wanted to cut their own trees. The other was just a thirty-minute trek around the property under the stars.

And everyone came to the s'mores table.

Calvin grinned up from where he stood poking marshmallows onto toasting forks. "Yep. Thanks for letting me help again."

"I couldn't do it without you. You're an integral part of the team." Cyan winked and started unwrapping the chocolate bars. "How was school this week?"

Calvin shrugged. "Okay, I guess."

"Learn anything useful?"

"Did you know two times two was four? It's the same as two plus two."

"That's cool. You like multiplying?" Cyan tried to remember when he started learning to multiply. Was it really second grade? Maybe it was. He'd been as excited about it as Calvin, though.

"It's neat. But I don't like spelling."

"Yeah? I always thought spelling was kind of fun. It's like a code. You already know the sounds letters make, 'cause you can read, right?"

Calvin nodded.

"So spelling is just like reading, but backwards. You have to take the word and break it out into the sounds. It can be tricky, though." Cyan shrugged. "Maybe it's still a little too hard."

Calvin frowned. "You really thought it was fun?"

"I did. I used to beat all my siblings at spelling."

"Really? Were you ever in a spelling bee?"

"Sort of." Did homeschool competitions count?

"There's a spelling bee at our school in February. The winner goes on to regionals and from there to state. I guess there's something bigger, too. It's not for losers?" Calvin's expression was a mixture of hope and scorn.

"Not to me. Unless I'm a loser?"

Calvin shook his head. "No way!"

Cyan chuckled. "Maybe I can help you practice?"

"Really?"

"Really." Voices and laughter carried over the open area toward them. "Sounds like our first group is headed this way. You've got the sticks loaded?"

"Yep. Should I put them in the fire?"

"Not yet. Might as well let them have the thrill. You want to help me get the chocolate onto the crackers?" Cyan gestured to the array of graham crackers he'd lined up like soldiers on plates on the table.

"How's my best boy?" Maria jogged up and ruffled Calvin's hair.

"Aw, Mom." Calvin rolled his eyes and glanced over at Cyan.

"You all set up?"

"We are. Only because I have the best helper around. Thanks for lending him to me." Cyan rested his hand on Calvin's shoulder. "You're not taking him yet, are you?"

Maria shook her head. "Nah. I thought I'd hang out here at the fire with you, though. It's cold tonight. And apparently I'm in the way at the sleigh ride sign up."

"How?" Wasn't that her assigned station? How could she be in the way?

"Betsy decided she wanted to be out tonight." Maria shrugged. "Gives me a chance to stay closer to the chocolate. And the warm."

Calvin giggled and broke a piece of chocolate off the bar near him. "Here, Mom."

"Thanks, baby." She slipped the square into her mouth and hummed. "Nothing better."

Cyan made a mental note to get Maria some chocolate. Maybe it'd pave the way to more time on the couch after Calvin headed to bed. He'd only made one other evening this week—though he'd purchased an e-copy of the book and had followed along as best he could on his own—and Maria was strict about making sure he was out the door as soon as Calvin headed off to brush his teeth. Not that he blamed her, really. The more he read in his Bible about God's expectations for His followers, the less sure he was that he'd ever be able to measure up.

"What?" Maria glanced at him, eyebrow raised.

"Sorry." Had he been staring? Calvin didn't seem to have noticed. That was good. "Do you ever feel like living up to Jesus' expectations is impossible?"

"Sure. They kind of are, if you're trying to do it on your own."

Cyan frowned. "What do you mean?"

"Just that it's not up to us to live a holy life. If we were able to do it on our own, we wouldn't need Jesus in the first place. We're only able to do it—at any level—when we let the Holy Spirit work in us. Then we change, and what we want aligns more with God's desire than our own selfish ones."

Huh. Still seemed impossible. How was he supposed to tell the difference between his desires and the ones God said it was okay for him to have? Like wanting more of a relationship with Maria. Was that from God? Or was it simply because he found her attractive and adored her son? Could it be both?

She touched his arm. "You're not going to figure it all out at once. It's a lifetime process."

"I was that obvious?"

Maria laughed. "I think every believer struggles with the idea at some point. Maybe a whole bunch of points. Just wait until you mess up and you have to work through feeling like you crossed lines Jesus can't—or won't—forgive you for."

Cyan watched Calvin offer toasting forks to the steady trickle of bundled up guests as they arrived from their sleigh rides. Had she considered Calvin in that light? That must've been awful. "I thought the whole point was that nothing like that existed."

"Sure it is." Maria adjusted the plates with graham crackers and chocolate. "Doesn't mean you don't feel that way sometimes."

He blew out a breath. Everything was always just a little harder than it seemed like it was going to be. Time to change the subject. "How long can I keep my helper tonight?"

Maria tugged her phone out of her coat pocket and pressed the button. The time lit up the screen. "Another hour?"

"That'll work. Thanks." The first of the toasters came over to the table with a pair of blackened marshmallows on their fork. "Hi. Ready for chocolate?"

"Yes, please."

Cyan helped scoot the sticky, charred mess onto the waiting s'mores pieces. "Cal? Here's a fork to clean and reload."

Calvin darted over. For whatever reason, this was the kid's favorite part. Or so he claimed. As far as Cyan was concerned, he was welcome to it. All that stickiness? Yuck.

Maria drifted toward the fire and spoke to several of the people who were busy making their own treats. It was a smallish community. It probably made sense that she knew a lot of the folks who included a trip to the ranch as part of their Christmas tradition. Would he ever fit in like that?

A man laughed and grabbed her around the waist.

Cyan took a step forward and rammed his leg into the table.

Maria darted a look over her shoulder before stepping out of the man's grasp. Was it the glow of the firelight giving her cheeks their red tint? She patted his shoulder and moved to another clump of people.

Cyan worked to steady his breathing. It had been a long time since he'd wanted to slam his fist into someone's face.

The man wandered over to the table and shot Cyan an evaluating glance. "You're Cyan?"

He nodded. "Ready for chocolate?"

"Oh, no, I don't eat s'mores. I come up with the singles group from church because it's a fun outing and a chance to see Maria. She never joins our activities." There was a hint of suspicion in his voice. "Known her long?"

"Just since Thanksgiving when I came to visit my grandparents." Did it matter how long they'd known each other? If he'd known Maria longer but she still didn't want anything to do with him, wasn't that her choice? "But we've been spending a lot of time together."

"She mentioned that." The man sighed and the bluster in his posture disappeared. "She deserves to have a good man. Don't let her down."

Cyan tried to form a response, but no words came. He'd try, but how was he supposed to promise that? Hadn't he already let her down a little with this upcoming work trip? And there was no way around that. He had to go.

The man just stared. Was he waiting for an answer?

"I'll do my best."

After a moment, he nodded and stuck out his hand. "I'm Trent."

"Cyan. Nice to meet you?"

Trent laughed and shook his head. "No, it isn't, but it's nice of you to say. I'm not really a jerk."

"Okay."

Trent laughed again. "I think you and I are going to be friends. Even if you end up marrying Maria out from under me."

"Were you dating?"

"Ouch." Trent pointed his finger at Cyan. "See? Quick wit, well-timed burns. Definitely friend material. But, to answer the question, no. We never dated. Not for lack of asking on my part. She says I'm not her type."

"Maybe we can be friends."

Trent grinned. "You're coming to church with the Hewitts, right? Hit up our small group after service some time. Maybe you can drag Maria along. I know her kid goes to one—not sure where she goes, though."

"She goes to the same group my grandparents attend while *Calvin* is at Sunday school." It shouldn't make him bristle to hear someone call Cal *her kid*, but it did.

Trent considered a moment before nodding. "That explains it."

"What?"

"The kid—um, Calvin. I'm not good with them, I can admit that. I probably give off a vibe. No mom's going to date someone like that, are they?"

Cyan shrugged. Probably not, but who knew what some moms would do? "Not one who isn't into dating for the sake of dating."

"All right, I concede the field. Not that I was ever actually on it." Trent looked over at where Calvin was busy cleaning and reloading toasting forks as the group turned them in. "You really don't mind having a kid in the mix?"

"Mind? Calvin's worth knowing all on his own. His mom's just icing."

"Good line." Trent laughed.

Cyan frowned.

"Not a line. Got it." Trent held up his hands. "I think maybe I'll go before I dig myself another big hole. Still think we can be friends though, man. Keep it in mind."

Cyan watched him amble back toward the bonfire before glancing down at the nearly depleted s'mores making. He leaned over to get more plates and crackers.

Maria hurried to his side. "I'm so sorry. Trent is...he's just...he's harmless."

Cyan snorted. "That's not the word I'd choose."

"Was he mean? I can—"

"Nah, it's fine. I think we're good."

"Okay. He's always asking me out, and takes it fine when I say no. I don't know why I said I was seeing someone tonight." Her hands were working quickly to unwrap chocolate bars and snap them into pieces. She didn't meet his eyes.

"You did?"

Maria gave a slight nod.

Cyan grinned.

Her gaze slid over to him. "That's okay, right? To tell people?"

It was a miracle he didn't float straight off into the star-studded sky. "Absolutely."

"Okay. Good." She reached for another stack of plates. "I wasn't sure. You never act like we're anything other than friends when we're around your grandparents or the ranch guys. So, I thought maybe—"

"I thought that was what you wanted." Cyan reached over and grabbed her hand. He gave her a little tug so she stepped closer and their sides touched. "It's been killing me."

She looked up and their eyes met. Her voice was breathy. "Really?"

Cyan lowered his lips to hers. "Really."

12

Maria closed the oven door and checked the time. They'd settled into a routine with Cyan over the last week and a half. Tonight, she was going to try and shake things up a little. So she'd invited him to supper.

"I thought you said the shells were too much hassle for weekdays." Calvin looked up from where he was doing homework at the kitchen table.

Heat flooded Maria's cheeks. She had, in fact, told Calvin that. More than once. They were a lot of work. But they were always something people complimented when she did serve them. "How's your homework going?"

Calvin sighed. "Homework is stupid. Why do we have to do it the week before Christmas?"

"Because, if they gave you the week before Christmas off, then everyone would ask why they had to do homework the week before the week they got off. And then so on and so on, until no one ever did any work and people would stop knowing how to read and the world would devolve into chaos."

Calvin giggled. "Mo-om."

"What?" Maria crossed the kitchen and drilled a finger into Calvin's side. "Where did I go wrong?"

"You're silly." He bent back over the page. "Can I have two shells?"

"Why don't we start with one and see how hungry you still are after that?" She frantically tried to figure out the insulin that he'd need for two stuffed shells and the brownie sundaes she'd planned for after. Hopefully, he'd be happy with one, since that's what she'd planned. "Don't forget, I made dessert, too."

He perked up. "I get some?"

Maria's heart broke. Had she been too strict about sugar? She just wanted him to be safe. Healthy. "You get some."

Calvin slapped his notebook closed. "Finished. When do we eat?"

"As soon as it's ready. Maybe another half hour. Why don't you grab your book and you can read to me? Then we can check that off your list, too."

"Aww."

Maria shook her head and pointed. What was it going to take to get him to love to read? Everyone she talked to said it was a matter of finding the right books. There weren't a ton of options for seven-year-olds. He did, at least, enjoy listening when she read aloud. He liked it more when Cyan did it.

Calvin shuffled over to the couch and flopped dejectedly onto it. He flipped open the book and began to mutter the words.

The knock at the door forestalled any retort she was going to make.

"I'll get it!" Calvin tossed his book aside and flew across the room to grab the handle. "Cyan! It's not bedtime yet."

"Can I come in?" He grinned at Calvin, then glanced up and held Maria's gaze. A jolt sizzled through her. That was new. Ish.

"Hi. We're still about thirty minutes away from being ready. Sorry. I got a later start than I'd planned."

"Smells good." He glanced over at the couch and nodded at the book. "What're you reading?"

Calvin wrinkled his nose. "It's dumb."

"Calvin."

"Well, it is. And boring. But I have to read for thirty minutes every day anyway."

"Yeah?" Cyan picked up the book and flipped it over. "Doesn't sound so bad to me. Why don't you read me a chapter? Maybe I can borrow it when you're finished."

"Reading is for girls." Calvin sighed and trudged back to the couch. He took the book and found his place again.

"What? No way. I love to read. So does my grandpa. And my dad. And my brother, for that matter. Reading is for people who want to be smart." Cyan stretched his arm out on the back of the couch so it was behind Calvin. "I bet your mom reads."

"I love to read, as it happens." Maria dried her hands on a towel and joined them on the couch. Would Cyan's input help turn the tide? As much as she'd love to see Calvin reading without whining about it, was it wise to let him get dependent on Cyan? She wanted him in their lives—and he would be. Sort of. After he got back from New York. Before he had to go somewhere else. Would he have to? He talked like this thing in New York was unusual. But how often would it happen?

"That's 'cause she's a girl. All the girls in class read too, and they make fun of anyone who says a word wrong."

Uh oh. "That's not very nice of them."

Calvin shook his head. "Mrs. Perez never hears it, either, so they don't get in trouble. None of the boys like to read aloud now."

Maria made a mental note to send his teacher an email after he went to bed. That simply wasn't acceptable.

"Well, you read and I promise not to laugh or make any comments. Then, maybe it'll be time for you to show me how to set the table." Cyan slid his arm onto the back of the couch, brushing his fingers across Maria's neck.

Calvin sighed and started reading. At least it wasn't a mutter anymore.

Maria let her head relax against the top of the cushion. How nice it would be to end every night this way.

As Calvin got to the last page of his chapter, the oven timer buzzed.

"Is it ready?" Calvin slapped the book shut, grinning. "Mom's stuffed shells are the best. But she only makes them for special occasions. Are you a special occasion, Mr. Cyan?"

He chuckled. "That'd be nice, wouldn't it? Maybe we're celebrating the last Tuesday before Christmas. That's a pretty special day, you know."

"Yeah? Why?" Calvin jumped off the couch and moved a stool in the kitchen so he could climb up to reach the plates. He handed Cyan three of them and hopped down.

Cyan set the plates on the table. "Um. Because it means we're less than eight days away?"

Calvin giggled. "You're as silly as Mom. Here, I'll get cups if you can do the silverware. I never remember which side the fork goes on."

"When you're finished with that, we need to check your blood sugar and do your insulin." Maria set the pan of stuffed shells in the center of the table. It'd be nice not to have to stab him with a syringe so many times throughout the day. They were finding a rhythm, but it wasn't easy. Or fun.

Cyan finished setting the table while Maria handled Calvin's medication. Finished, they all took their seats. The three of them around the table was like a family. Her heart gave a funny little skip in her chest. Was it wrong to pray for more than one miracle at a time? She was already begging God to make a way for them to afford the insulin pump. Was it greedy to hope He'd make a way for Calvin to have a complete family, too?

"What do you want for Christmas?" Maria fought the urge to snuggle up against Cyan and, instead, tucked her feet under her and leaned against the arm of the sofa.

"I don't really need anything." Cyan stretched his arm along the back of the couch and brushed her shoulder with his fingers. "I could use some help decorating my cabin."

She ignored the shivers his touch caused. "That's no fun. I'll help you decorate now. Although, you need to remember your promise to redo that kitchen. It's...tragic. Decorating help isn't going to fix it."

He chuckled and shifted, inching closer. "Maybe if I wait long enough, that gold will come back in fashion."

"No." She shook her head. "Even if it does, just no."

"All right, if you're sure." His voice was teasing and his eyes sparked with laughter. "Thanks for dinner. It was incredible."

"I'm glad you liked it." She was glad about a lot of things. Calvin's blood sugar after dinner was right where it needed to be, even with a brownie for dessert. "Thanks for staying after Cal went to bed."

"I can't think of any place I'd rather be."

Her cheeks heated. "You say things like that a lot. A girl could get the wrong idea."

"I don't think it'd be the wrong idea. I like you. I like spending time with you, both alone and with Calvin. I want this to grow into something more between us."

"More. Like what?"

"Love. Marriage. Maybe more kids, if that's something you're interested in."

She drew in a shaky breath. "And if I'm not?"

"Then I guess we'll talk about it, and I'll try to convince you you're wrong." Cyan flashed a grin. "I can be persuasive when I need to be."

Maria laughed. "I just bet. As it happens, I've always wanted more kids, but dating when you've already got one is harder than it seems. At least if you're trying to do it God's way."

"So?"

"So, what?"

"I guess I'd like to know how far off base I am. I don't see you inviting anyone else over for stuffed shells and bedtime stories, so I know there's something here. But how big is it? Do we have a chance? Even with me leaving in January? I know that's not what you prefer."

Right. He was still leaving. Which meant what? Nothing. It didn't mean anything, really, other than that they'd have to take things slow. Wasn't that what she wanted anyway? "I just...long distance relationships are hard. And what if you end up loving it and decide to stay?"

Cyan laughed. "Never going to happen. I don't like the city. I like it here. And I think you're worth a little extra effort. I know it's not going to be easy, but that doesn't change wanting to make it work."

Every word was exactly the right one. She closed her eyes and searched her heart, praying that God would make it obvious if this wasn't what He wanted. When nothing immediate came to mind, she opened her eyes and met his gaze. "You're not off base. I want all those same things. Love. Marriage. More kids. With you."

Cyan grinned and closed the distance between them. He pulled her onto his lap and buried his face against her neck.

Maria melted into his embrace.

It felt like home.

13

Cyan padded barefoot into the kitchen. He frowned when he found it empty. Seeing Maria in the kitchen had quickly become one of the highlights of his morning. Crossing to the coffee pot, he poured a mug, doctored it, and carried it with him as he peeked into the pantry and dining room. Where was she?

He headed to his grandparents' office and tapped on the door frame. Wayne looked up from the computer and grinned.

"Morning. Sleep well?"

"I did. Have you seen Maria?"

Wayne shook his head. "I can fix you some breakfast if you're hungry."

"No. That's not what I was angling for. I can grab a bowl of cereal. I—she didn't say anything about being late today, did she?"

"It's not like we punch a clock. I'm sure she'll turn up when she's finished whatever it is that's holding her up."

"You're right." Cyan sipped his coffee and pushed aside the rest of worry that threatened to crawl up his throat. "Maybe I'll grab that cereal."

"All right." Wayne smiled and gave a half-hearted wave as he turned back to the computer.

Cyan wandered back to the kitchen and frowned again. He looked out the window above the sink at Maria's cabin. Where was her car? He slipped his phone out of his pocket and tapped Maria's contact. He drummed his fingers on the counter as it rang.

"Cyan, hi. What's up?"

His eyebrows lifted. What was the beeping in the background. "I was wondering where you were. Your car is gone?"

Her breath crackled in his ear. "Yeah, sorry. I left a voicemail for Betsy. We're at the hospital."

His heart clutched. "Calvin? He's okay?"

"He will be."

It was like pulling teeth. "What happened?"

"I woke up around two because he was moaning. I couldn't get him to respond, or wake up enough to even swallow juice to try and get his blood sugar back up. We're not sure why it dropped like it did—he was fine when he went to bed. I must have calculated something wrong. The doctors have all said it happens, especially when the diagnosis is new."

"Why didn't you call me? I would've come with you."

"Didn't you hear me say two a.m.? Besides, he's not your son. He's my responsibility."

That was true. Unkind, perhaps, but still true. Did she not realize he loved Calvin? He couldn't keep the ice from his voice. "Right. Of course."

Maria sighed. "Look, I left a message for Betsy and asked her to let you know. I'm sorry she didn't get to you."

"How hard would it have been to just text me yourself?" The words were out before he could stop them.

"I didn't want to risk you waking up. You didn't need to come with us. There was no need to disturb you."

He should quit while he was behind. Except... "Just last night we were talking about the future. Love. Marriage. More kids. In that scenario, were you figuring Calvin wouldn't also be mine? Am I only supposed to care about hypothetical children we make together?"

"That's not what I said."

"Isn't it?" Cyan ended the call and tossed his phone on the counter. What possible future was there between them if he wasn't allowed to consider Calvin his, too?

Betsy shuffled into the kitchen, offering a bright smile when she spotted him. "There you are. How'd you sleep?"

"Great. Fine." Cyan took a deep breath. Betsy wasn't to blame for any of this. He shouldn't take it out her. "Sorry. You?"

She rubbed his arm as she passed him on her way to the coffee pot. "I gather you spoke with Maria?"

He nodded.

"Maria seemed pretty low key in the voicemail, Calvin okay?"

Cyan shrugged. "I guess. All she'd say, aside from how he's not my responsibility, is that he'll be fine."

"I'm sure she didn't mean it like that, Cyan. She's stressed—give her some grace." Betsy frowned as she filled her mug. "And remember that she's been on her own for seven years."

"So obviously she should spit in the eye of anyone who tries to help."

"Oh, honey. That's not what she was doing, I'm sure."

Cyan snorted. He wasn't convinced. Betsy might know Maria better—they'd known each other longer, certainly—but it wasn't hard to interpret the situation. Not when Maria used clear, small words.

"Why don't you go on down to the hospital and see them in person? I'm positive she'd welcome a visit, and you can clear this up."

He shook his head. "I have work I need to do. Maybe later."

Betsy sighed. "Don't let it fester too long, okay?"

Cyan grabbed his phone and tucked it in his pocket. Better not to answer than to agree to something he wasn't sure he could promise. Maybe his grandmother was right and he needed to cut Maria a little slack. On the flip side, it wouldn't kill Maria to realize that a relationship meant two people. All the time.

Cyan clicked the radio button to get expedited shipping and submitted his order. He never had made the time to go into one of the bigger towns to shop. Maria had suggested a Sunday afternoon, and they'd tried, but life seemed to conspire against the trip. There was a lot of work that went on to make it possible to open things up for Christmas tree cutting, sleigh rides, and the campfires. So, online shopping it was. And since he still had five days before Christmas, everything should arrive with plenty of time.

He checked the time on the screen of his laptop. Close enough to a full day's work. He'd barely been able to focus, anyway, wondering about Calvin. And his mom.

He could text her. But there was no guarantee Maria would respond. Or, if she did, he might end up getting the spiel about how Calvin wasn't Cyan's responsibility. Then he'd throw his phone across the room and it would probably break, and a replacement phone wasn't really an inconvenience he wanted to deal with right now. That left heading into town, to the hospital, and working really hard not to show how mad he still was about the whole situation.

Cyan closed the lid of his computer and pushed back from the dining room table. If he wasn't going to get any more work done, he might as well take that drive. If nothing else, he could see Calvin for himself. That would alleviate some worry.

Cyan shook his head as he stomped into his boots and bundled into his coat. They hadn't had any fresh snow in over a week, but nothing was melting, either. It was definitely winter in the mountains. Why hadn't he imagined New Mexico would have snow? Probably because the word Mexico drummed up visions of hot, sandy beaches and Aztec ruins, not snowy mesas. His brain never changed that, even with the addition of the word "New" and several hundred miles north.

Before long, Cyan was outside Calvin's hospital room door, his stomach twisted into knots. Maybe this was a bad idea.

"You can go on in." The nurse he'd checked in with nodded toward the door. "He's not sleeping."

"Right. Thanks." Cyan smiled and tapped on the door before heading in.

Maria glanced up, her finger marking the spot on the page of the book she'd been reading aloud. "Cyan."

"Hi." He tucked his hands in his pockets. Not the warmest greeting in the world, but what was he supposed to say? He looked over at Calvin. "Hey, champ. How're you feeling?"

"I'm better. I want to go home." His mouth slid into a pout. "Mom says I have to stay overnight."

"I'm sure that's what the doctors said, too." Cyan moved to perch on the side of the bed.

"Nuh-uh. They said I could go this afternoon if everything stayed stable, but that if it made Mom feel better they'd keep me overnight."

"Calvin." Maria's voice was tinged with exasperation. "You were really sick last night. I don't want to risk a repeat."

"How come I have to stay here just because you're scared? It's dumb." Calvin crossed his arms. "And this book is dumb. Diabetes is dumb. *You're* dumb."

"Calvin." Maria stood, setting the book aside before moving to his bed. "That's no way to talk."

Calvin shrugged and turned away from his mom.

Maria took a deep breath and stared at the ceiling. Was she fighting tears? She had to be exhausted—mentally and physically.

"Maria? Why don't you go downstairs and get a coffee? Take a little break. I can hang out with Calvin for a bit, so he won't be alone."

She shook her head. "I couldn't ask you to do that."

"You didn't. I offered." Was she so stubborn she couldn't see a friendly offer when it was given?

"You don't have to—"

"Just stop. I wouldn't have suggested it if it wasn't something I was happy to do, but maybe you'd rather I left?"

"No. Mr. Cyan, you just got here." It was the closest to a whine he'd heard from Calvin since he'd known the boy. "Can't you stay a little bit? You could read. Then at least the animals would have voices."

Cyan winced and glanced at Maria.

Her shoulders fell. "Fine. I have my cell if you need me."

"I'm so—"

"Don't, okay?" Maria grabbed her purse and brushed past him on the way out the door.

"You need to give your mom a break, bud. This is hard on her."

Calvin frowned. "She's not the one stuck in the dumb hospital. I missed the Thanksgiving party and now I'm gonna miss the Christmas one, too, and I shouldn't have to."

"She's stuck here, too, you know. 'Cause she loves you."

"I guess."

Cyan chuckled. "I know it. You've got a good mom, kiddo. She does everything for you all on her own. That's not easy. She's brave and strong and smart."

Calvin sighed. "I just want to go home. The doctor told Mom some kind of pump would make it easier, but she said we can't afford it. That's du—"

"Dumb. Got it. We should work on some other adjectives. You're smart like your mom. You should have a better vocabulary."

"Mom says I can't say stupid."

Cyan smothered a smile. Maria probably wasn't on board with dumb then, either. Calvin would most likely figure that out before long. "Want me to read?"

Calvin shrugged.

Taking it for assent, Cyan settled in the chair by the bed and found the place where Maria had been reading. They were nearly finished with the book. Did she already have the next in the series? As he began to read, he considered the problem of the pump. Insurance companies could take time—they were the embodiment of bureaucracy—but surely there was a way to get the device without dealing with insurance. Of course, it might mean Maria had to accept someone's help. Was she capable of doing that?

"I brought you a coffee, too." Maria glanced over at the bed and a tiny smile tugged at her lips. "He fell asleep."

"I made it about half a chapter. After the long night you had, I'm not surprised." Cyan reached for the coffee. "Thanks for this. Can I ask you something?"

Wariness crept over her features and she perched on the edge of Calvin's bed. "Okay?"

"Why doesn't he have an insulin pump?"

She shook her head. "Insurance. I've appealed their denial, but that takes time. So we'll wait."

"And if they don't overturn the original decision?"

Maria shrugged. "I have to believe they will. God knows we need the thing. He's going to get it for us."

That was an opening. His heart raced. "What if I got it for you?"

"No. There's no possible way. Do you have any idea how expensive they are?"

"You've mentioned it. I have money. I can't think of anything I'd rather spend it on." Cyan set the coffee aside and leaned forward. "Let me help you. Let me help *him*."

"I don't—I can't—why would you offer that?" Maria shifted and laid her hand on Calvin's foot.

Everything in him deflated. She didn't understand at all. Their conversation the night before—marriage, a family— how could that happen if he wasn't allowed to share what he had with her? Maybe it was early in their relationship. If he worked hard at it, he could almost see that possibility, but at what point would she let him in? Would it be before they were married? After? How long after? "Why wouldn't I? I have the ability to help two people I care about. How is that wrong?"

"I didn't say it was wrong. It's just—he's not your responsibility."

"You keep saying that. What if I want him to be? Did you listen to me last night at all?" He reached out and touched her knee. "I care about you. I care about Calvin. Why does it matter if I help you now, before we're married?"

"Married is down the road. Somewhere." Maria's voice ended in a squeak.

Cyan frowned. "I thought we agreed it was where we were headed."

"Headed. That's different."

"How?"

"It just is. I mean, I'm not going to sleep with you just because we're headed toward marriage."

"That's not the same thing at all, and you know it."

Maria jerked one shoulder in a grumpy shrug.

Cyan surged to his feet. He clenched his teeth together in an attempt to keep from shouting and waking up Calvin. "You realize you don't have to do everything yourself, don't you? There are people who want to help. People who love you. But you throw that back at them and spit in their faces. And Calvin's the one who suffers."

Maria paled. Her mouth opened.

Cyan held up a hand. "Don't. Just don't. Tell Calvin I hope to see him back home really soon."

He stalked from the hospital room. She was never going to change. Never going to let anyone else in. And if that was the case, how could they have any sort of future together?

14

Maria and Calvin slipped into the back row at the Christmas Eve service.

Calvin tugged on the sleeve of Maria's sweater. "Mr. Cyan is up there, with Mrs. Hewitt and Mr. Hewitt. Why can't we sit up there?"

"There's not room. We're okay back here, right bud?" Her heart sank. She'd had a half-formed hope that the three of them would have chosen to attend a different service. Of course, they always attended this one, so there was no reason for them to have changed just because she was trying to avoid Cyan. It wasn't wrong to have turned down his offer. It was a lot of money, and money like that always had strings attached to it, didn't it? If the insurance ending up turning them down, again, she'd find a way to handle it on her own. One way or another. She could defer her school for a few semesters and turn the tuition into medical payments. There were options. Options that would let her handle her responsibilities on her own.

"It doesn't look crowded, Mom. Please?"

"No, Calvin. We're fine here. You'll get to see them tomorrow at lunch." Unless she could figure out some way to avoid it. That, of course, was impossible seeing as how she was in charge of making and serving all the food. She wouldn't even have the benefit of a large party at the table. None of the ranch hands were coming. Tommy was out of town for a day or two visiting his daughter. His ex-wife seemed to be adept at keeping the child from coming to the ranch to visit and, instead, requiring Tommy to travel if he wanted to exercise his visitation. Morgan was spending the day with friends from church, and Joaquin had invited a few friends to something informal at his cabin. He was a good cook, when he took the time, so there'd be no hardship there. And so, she and Calvin would be stuck spending Christmas day with the Hewitts. With Cyan.

Calvin's elbow dug into her side, dragging her out of her thoughts. Everyone was rising to their feet. Maria hastily shrugged out of her coat, draped it over the back of her seat, tucked her purse by her feet, and stood. She joined in singing *What Child is This?* and slipped her arm around Calvin's shoulder. Tonight was about celebrating the birth of Jesus, not worrying about Cyan and his extravagant, outrageous offer. The one she could never hope to repay. The one she should, without a question, continue to refuse. The one she yearned for with all her heart.

Maria glanced down at Calvin and shook her head. The insurance would come through. It had to. Didn't it? Something had to lift the cloud that hovered over her son, and had since Thanksgiving. They'd learn to live with diabetes. People did. But a pump would make it so much easier. And yet, accepting Cyan's offer to pay for it stuck uncomfortably in her chest. How could she accept such a huge thing from him?

But if she didn't, where did that leave her and Cyan?

She sank to her seat with the crowd and watched the pastor approach the pulpit.

"Tonight, I want to talk to you about the greatest gift you can ever receive. If you've been around church long, you're probably trying to figure out a way to yawn without everyone around you noticing. That's okay, I get it. Sometimes I think Christians say the same things so often that we forget the power of their truth. But here we are, the night before Christmas, and I wouldn't be doing my job if I let you go home without reminding you that Jesus—God made flesh—came to Earth for the sole purpose of dying on the cross so that you and I could be forgiven and our relationship with God restored. If that isn't the greatest gift available to everyone on this planet, then I'm missing something." The pastor paused and took a tiny sip of water.

Calvin shifted in his seat and let his head drop to Maria's shoulder. Was he low or just a seven-year-old in a sermon? She reached into her purse and dug out the blood testing kit. She pricked his finger and squeezed a drop of blood onto the strip, fighting the urge to tap her foot while it calculated his blood sugar.

Hm. Ninety-six. Not low. Technically. But he'd been higher than that when they left home, which suggested his levels were dropping. She reached for her purse and dug out a butterscotch candy and offered it to him. Calvin grinned and unwrapped it, popping it in his mouth.

Maria turned her attention back to the pastor.

"One of the reasons we give gifts at Christmas is to remind one another of the love of Christ. So, as much I urge you to work to keep from getting caught up in the gift giving and receiving, I'll also encourage you to accept, with grace, gifts that are given. Don't look for an even exchange. Instead, use your gifts as an expression of God's love, and accept the gifts given as a reminder of it. God loved us so much, that He gave us His Son…"

Maria looked down at her hands, tuning out the rest of the sermon. She'd already received so many extravagant gifts in her life. Salvation, though she'd ignored it for many years as a teen. The love and acceptance of the Hewitts. Calvin. How could she deserve more?

How could she deserve Cyan and everything he offered?

Maria tucked the blanket up around Calvin's shoulders and kissed his forehead. "Good night, baby. Sleep well."

"Night, Mama. Merry Christmas." Calvin grinned, though his eyes were sleepy. "Can't I stay up a little later?"

She chuckled and shook her head. "It'll be morning before you know it."

"Waffles! And presents?"

"We'll have to see, won't we?"

Calvin sighed. "There's always presents on Christmas morning. Even though we hafta wait until lunch to do Christmas with Mr. Hewitt and Mrs. Hewitt."

"Is that so?"

"Mooom."

Maria laughed and kissed his nose. "If you know everything, why do you ask?"

"Just making sure." Calvin wiggled deeper into his pillow. "I love you. So so much."

Her heart swelled. She'd never get tired of hearing it. "I love *you* so so much. I'll see you in the morning."

Turning off the light as she left the room, Maria pulled the door so it was almost closed behind her and let her shoulders slump. They'd run into everyone from the ranch at the punch and cookie gathering after the Christmas Eve service. Cyan had sent her a few questioning looks, but had otherwise been friendly, like nothing had ever happened between them. Including the kisses.

Were they back to square one?

She filled a mug with water at the tap and stuck it in the microwave. She was half-tempted to go to bed herself, but she'd just toss and turn. When her water was hot, she dropped a chamomile tea bag into it and carried it to the sofa. The room was dim, lit only by the Christmas tree and the light over the stove in the kitchen. Before she could settle completely, there was a quiet tap at the door.

With a sigh, she set her mug on the end table and padded over. Her eyebrows drew together as she tugged open the door. "Cyan?"

"Hi." He wasn't wearing a coat. He tucked his hands in his pockets as one corner of his mouth quirked up. "Can I come in?"

"Sure, I guess." She stepped back and reached for the light switch. Her heart hammered against her ribs and she fought to keep her movements from becoming jerky as she went back to her tea.

Cyan perched on the edge of the couch, his knees angled so they almost bumped hers. "I've decided to head to New York early."

"What? Why?" Maria wrapped her hands around the mug and held it close to her chest.

"I—it seemed like maybe you could use some space. Away from me, I mean. Here, at the ranch, we're always going to run into one another." He paused and ran a hand through his hair. "It hurts, knowing I've made you feel uncomfortable in your own space. I'll apologize for that. Not for offering to get the pump for Calvin—although, it would be as much for you as for him—but I wasn't trying to hurt you by suggesting it."

"You didn't hurt me." Scared her, maybe.

He lifted a shoulder. "It got awkward, anyway. And that was never my intention."

"I don't want you to go." The words were out before she fully registered she'd intended to say them. Before she realized how true they were.

Cyan angled his head to the side, his eyes holding hers. "You don't?"

Barely able to catch her breath, she shook her head.

"I guess I'm confused."

Maria couldn't stop her chuckle, though she wished it didn't have a hint of desperation clinging to the corners. She set her tea on the end table and reached for his hand. "I'm sorry. I've handled this all so badly. I—if you really want to buy the pump. If you can, without it being a hardship, I'd appreciate it. And I don't know how to thank you. It's hard for me, because I have all these feelings for you, feelings I promised myself I'd never have for someone again, and yet there they were."

"Were?" His eyes shuttered.

"Are." Maria swallowed. It was time to accept the gifts that God sent her way. "I love you, Cyan. I know Calvin feels the same. And I—we—want you in our lives. Not because of money you spend on us or anything like that, just because you're you."

A smile bloomed on his lips, his eyes crinkling at the corners and lighting from inside. "You have no idea how much I want to hear that."

She did, actually. He hadn't said it back. Maybe her response to the pump made him need more time? She'd give it to him. Even if it killed her.

Cyan reached into his back pocket and drew out an envelope. "This is for you."

Frowning, she looked down at the simple scrawl of her name then back up at Cyan.

"I was just going to leave it with Betsy to give you later. Or throw away." He tentatively took her hand. "It's a letter telling you I love you. Asking if you and Calvin will come visit me at spring break. I was hoping time might make you realize you felt the same about me as I did you."

"You love me?" A tear slipped down Maria's cheek. Then another.

"I really do." He scooted closer and wrapped her in his arms.

Maria burrowed into his chest. "I don't deserve you."

"Didn't you listen to the pastor at all tonight?" With one finger, Cyan tipped her chin up so their eyes met. "The best gifts? The ones that matter most? They're not the ones we can earn."

"Like Jesus."

Cyan nodded and lowered his head so their lips brushed. "And love."

Acknowledgements

Thanks so much for reading *Hope for Christmas*! I hope you enjoyed reading about Cyan and Maria as they start down the path to love. Novellas are always a challenge for me. I very much want to give my readers, and my characters, that happily ever after ending that's always so satisfying, but it's hard to do in such a short space of time. Because of that, we didn't get a ring at the end of this story, but you'll see much more of these two in future books in the Ranch of Hope series. I hope you'll stick around for that!

As always, I owe a huge debt of thanks to my husband and sons for giving me the time and space I need to write. They're always so supportive and often shoo me out of the house when I need to get words down. Thanks also go to Valerie Comer for being an extraordinary critique partner and, more delightfully, friend. I'm blessed to have you in my life. Thanks also to Kimberly Johnson for organizing this Christmas box and allowing me to participate.

Thanks also to my heavenly Father for sending us Jesus so that we can have a relationship with Him. I'm so grateful for His grace in my life and for the stories that He continues to allow to form in my mind.

Finally, but by no means least, thank YOU for reading. While it's entirely likely I'd continue to write books if everyone stopped reading them, it's so much nicer to know that the characters I love are getting a chance to meet and spend time with the readers on the other side of the page.

About the Author

Elizabeth Maddrey is a semi-reformed computer geek and homeschooling mother of two who lives in the suburbs of Washington D.C. When she isn't writing, Elizabeth is a voracious consumer of books. She loves to write about Christians who struggle through their lives, dealing with sin and receiving God's grace on their way to their own romantic happily ever after. You can find out more and sign up to receive her newsletter at http://www.ElizabethMaddrey.com and interact with her at http://www.Facebook.com/ElizabethMaddrey

If you enjoyed *Hope for Christmas*, you'd also enjoy Cyan's older sister, Azure. You can read about her in *A Heart Realigned*, book 3 in my Peacock Hill Romance series.

https://www.amazon.com/dp/B07DSR5LX6

She has no roots. He has no wings.

Repainting historic murals at Peacock Hill will pad Azure Hewitt's bank account and allow her to drift where the wind takes her. If only the group of friends working at the old mansion weren't so welcoming. Their immediate acceptance and inclusion reinforces one of the downsides of her footloose life. Add in the local car buff and mechanic? Putting down roots could almost be attractive.

The more Matt Patterson's uncle pushes him to take over the family auto shop, the less Matt's sure he wants to stay where he's planted…but even as he contemplates spreading his wings, he can't imagine a life like Azure's with no fixed address. Even so, he's positive a settled life isn't something she sees in her future.

With Azure's project nearing completion and Matt's uncle anxious for a decision, neither is sure where God is calling them to be. But if their hearts are aligned to His desire, surely their love will have a chance.